POISON AT THE VILLAGE SHOW

MARTHA MILLER COSY MYSTERIES – BOOK ONE

CATHERINE COLES

Boldwood

First published in Great Britain in 2022 by Boldwood Books Ltd.

Cover Design by CC Book Design

Cover Photography: Shutterstock

A CIP catalogue record for this book is available from the British Library.

Paperback ISBN 978-1-80415-063-4

Large Print ISBN 978-1-80415-059-7

Hardback ISBN 978-1-80415-058-0

Ebook ISBN 978-1-80415-056-6

Kindle ISBN 978-1-80415-057-3

Audio CD ISBN 978-1-80415-064-1

MP3 CD ISBN 978-1-80415-061-0

Digital audio download ISBN 978-1-80415-055-9

Boldwood Books Ltd
23 Bowerdean Street
London SW6 3TN
www.boldwoodbooks.com

For my brother, who I miss every day, but whose loss reminds me how important it is to continually reach for your dreams and never, ever give up

CHARACTER LIST

Martha Miller – Protagonist
Ruby Andrews – Martha's sister
Luke Walker – The new vicar
Alice Warren – Chairwoman of the Westleham Village Committee
Charles Warren – Alice's husband
PC Cyril Bottomley – Village policeman
DI Ben Robertson – Police detective inspector
Ernest Harrington – Owner of post office and village shop
Elsie Harrington – Ernest's wife
George Felton – Villager
Gertrude Felton – George's wife and the vicarage housekeeper
Ada Garrett – Village gossip
Maud Burnett – Martha's neighbour, loves to repeat gossip
Joe Noble – Owner of the village pub, the Cricketer's Arms
Florence Noble – Joe's daughter
Margaret Leaming – Secretary of the Westleham Village Committee

Doctor Briggs – Village GP
John Bennington – Local farmer
Stan Miller – Martha's husband; disappeared a year ago
Lizzie – Martha's dog
Nancy Turner – Harringtons' nanny

ciency is with the housework,' I informed Lizzie mournfully. 'If only I were more like Ruby.'

'You would hate my job.' Ruby shuffled into the kitchen and pushed her stockinged feet into the slippers I put in front of the Aga to warm. 'It's tedious, exceedingly poorly paid and being on my feet all day cannot be good for my posture.'

'I didn't hear you come in.' I put on oven gloves and transferred the quiche I had left cooling on top of the Aga into the middle of the table next to a bowl of mixed salad.

'Perhaps if you weren't talking to the dog, you would have heard me.' Ruby gestured at Lizzie and rubbed the animal's head.

'I don't have anyone else to talk to all day.' I spread my hands out, palms up. 'And, besides, she never answers me back.'

'You really don't need to warm my slippers, Martha. It's July!' Ruby grinned at me before washing her hands.

I shrugged. 'I know your feet hurt after being on them all day. Warm slippers are a comfort.'

Ruby dried her hands and sat in the seat opposite me. Lizzie lay under the table near our feet. 'Thank you. They will comfort my feet for the next half an hour while I eat. Then I'm going out.'

I stifled a sigh. It wasn't Ruby's fault she was the complete opposite to me – she was bright, vivacious and incredibly beautiful. She went out each Friday and Saturday evening, though she never shared the details of her dates with me; we did not have that type of sisterly relationship.

I was the eldest sibling and still mortified I had to ask my younger sister to live with me so I had a chance of keeping up payments on the house. The need to take in a lodger was not what I had expected when I married a safe and responsible man like Stan.

A few weeks after my husband's disappearance, the manager at the local bank telephoned and summoned me to his office. He officiously explained that I could not access Stan's account for any reason, including withdrawal of funds, because it was in his sole name, but I could pay money in to cover the household bills.

Pay money in?

My cheeks burned as I remembered the humiliation of explaining I had no money of my own, and no way of earning any. During the war, I worked for the Women's Land Army but, of course, when the men returned home, women were no longer required to work the land.

After Stan left and a fruitless search for employment, my only option was to take in a lodger. I was fortunate I had a sister, who jumped at the chance of moving from the midlands to live nearer to the bright lights of London. Goodness only knows what would have become of me if Ruby hadn't come to my rescue.

'Do you have a date?' I asked as I cut the quiche and placed a slice on Ruby's plate.

'Yes.' Ruby nodded as she heaped lettuce, spinach, beetroot, radishes and tomatoes onto her plate. 'I'm going to the pictures.'

'With a man?' I poured us both a cup of tea and pushed Ruby's saucer across the table towards her. I rarely asked questions, but tonight it seemed I was more aware than normal of the lack of excitement in my own life.

'Yes.' Ruby's eyes met mine briefly, then she looked back down at her plate. 'I hear the new vicar is jolly nice-looking.'

'How do you know?'

Ruby waved a hand in the air. '*Everyone* is talking about it.'

Of course they were. The last exciting thing that happened in Westleham was when the previous vicar had keeled over before finishing his sermon. Doctor Briggs, our village physician, assured the congregation the vicar was dead before he hit the unforgiving stone floor of the church.

On second thoughts, 'exciting' probably wasn't the right word.

I bit my lip. Poor Reverend Gibbs. 'It'll be strange having a vicar who isn't old. Though I don't suppose the new fellow will have as much life experience to put into his sermons.'

'It is my belief that Reverend Gibbs put too much of everything into his sermons. Before I realised how serious the situation was, I thought he had bored himself to sleep.'

'Ruby!' I admonished, but couldn't help the corners of my mouth twitching up into a smile. She shrugged. 'What is in this quiche, Martha? It's delicious.'

'Spinach, spring onions, and peppers. Nothing fancy.'

We couldn't afford fancy. If I couldn't grow it in the garden or eke it out of the board Ruby paid me, we didn't have it. That was at least one good thing that had come out of the war. I had learned how to grow a whole host of fruit and vegetables. We also had chickens in our back garden. If Stan ever came home, it would have quite devastated him to see how my horticultural efforts had decimated the lawn he once prized so highly.

'Everything in your garden still intact?'

It was an innocent question, yet it didn't stop me from feeling incredibly guilty.

The village show was scheduled for tomorrow, and I was one of the few villagers whose garden had escaped unscathed. Someone, as yet unidentified, was entering gardens around the village in the dead of night and destroying plants.

'Yes. People are bound to point a finger at me and say I've ruined the competition to win a prize.' I almost wished the perpetrator would visit my garden and cause some damage so I wouldn't stand out. My untouched garden, full of its carefully grown produce, announced to the whole village that, thus far, I'd evaded the furtive vegetable killer and, no doubt, made them wonder if I was the guilty party.

'Your garden is simply the best.' Ruby reached over and

patted my hand. 'No one spends as much time tending their fruit and vegetables as you. Any prize you win will be well deserved.'

'Thank you,' I said, swallowing down the sudden lump in my throat. I concentrated on gathering the remains of the lettuce onto my fork while blinking away the moisture in my eyes. If Ruby knew how upset I was over the vandalism of village gardens, she wouldn't go out and leave me.

I had never been particularly sociable, even when Stan and I first moved to the village; I spent the early months of our marriage creating a home I hoped would make my husband happy. During the war, I was too busy to make friends. Afterwards, I had not enjoyed being the topic of village gossip when Stan disappeared. When I dug out the lawn to extend my small vegetable garden, I was devastated to discover one particularly nasty old lady named Ada Garrett had suggested I'd probably buried my husband under my potatoes.

Now, I was certain many of the villagers believed I was the person sneaking about in the dead of night, sabotaging other people's crops. But, first, I was so exhausted after a day in the garden, cleaning the kitchen after dinner and walking Lizzie to even think about leaving my cottage in the dead of night. Second, and of most importance, winning a rosette wasn't important to me in the slightest.

If, however, there was a monetary prize, I couldn't swear I wouldn't have happily hacked Mrs Henderson's succulent tomatoes or chopped Mr Peters' award-winning marrows in half.

* * *

I cleaned away the remnants of our meal and washed dishes whilst Ruby got ready for her date. The wireless blared noisily, the sounds of a modern tune I did not recognise floating down the stairs.

Not for the first time since Ruby had become my lodger, I felt old and disconnected with the world outside of Westleham. The last time I left the village was to take Lizzie to the vet. Which, of course, was another problem. My best friend was a dog.

Although I always had someone to talk to, every now and again, it would have been very nice to get a response that was not a wet muzzle or a conciliatory lick. I'd never been an emotional person, but more and more I had been craving human contact. Perhaps now I had started dealing with the financial implications of Stan's disappearance, I would be ready to examine my feelings about the incident that had shaped my life.

Shaking my head at my melancholy, I snapped on Lizzie's lead and pushed my feet into the shoes sitting forlornly next to the doormat. A human cuddle may well have been a very pleasant thought, but Ruby and I were not from a demonstrative family. My canine companion was my only option for comfort and that still made me much luckier than many after the devastation of the war.

I pushed the door closed behind me. Even if Ruby were out, I would have done the same. We did not live in the sort of community where locking one's front door was necessary. Stan, however, had always insisted on securing our home. I expect that was because he worked in London where, he informed me seriously, everyone was more suspicious of everyone else.

Usually, I turned to the left when I closed the garden gate behind me. I preferred to walk along the edge of Farmer Bennington's fields, where the chance of meeting other humans was non-existent.

Tonight, however, I walked towards the village. My home was on the edge of Westleham, set back from the quiet country lane that ran through the middle of the village. On either side of the gate were tall hedges that gave us a degree of privacy that we didn't really require. Our position in the village meant that people only walked this far down the lane when they wanted to visit us – which probably accounted for my melancholy mood: it was very rare for someone to knock on the door of Tulip Cottage.

My mouth quirked into a half-smile as I thought about the name for my home. Tulips were my favourite flower, but Stan hated the idea of our cottage having a plaque announcing its name. However, a few weeks after my husband's desertion, I struck a deal with John Bennington, the farmer who was my nearest neighbour to the east, and he made me a sign proclaiming the name of our home. I paid him in apple pies.

Since then, each time I returned home, I was reminded of the one act of rebellion in my marriage. How sad that I felt I had to wait until my husband had left me before I dared to do something of which I knew he would not have approved.

My nearest neighbour on the other side was Maud Burnett. She was an older lady who liked to listen to village gossip. Her greatest joy, however, was in repeating it. Maud was the person who informed me that Ada Garrett was telling villagers she was certain the police would not find Stan in London – but underneath my potatoes.

If I had been inclined to murder my husband, which I was not, I certainly would not have been silly enough to bury him on my own property. There were deep ditches between John Bennington's fields and the road; if one were to throw a body down there and cover it with leaves, it was unlikely to be discovered.

I shook my head. Perhaps the reason Ada spread such vile stories about me was because I looked guilty. I was certain ordinary housewives did not think of the best way to dispose of their husband. Though, in my defence, I had never had a single notion of doing away with Stan until he failed to come home that evening almost a year ago. Then I wished I was brave enough to bring about his disappearance by my own hand.

'Good evening!' a deep male voice called out.

I banished thoughts of Stan and murder and looked across the narrow lane. A dark-haired man I had never met before lifted a hand in greeting. In his other hand, he held a smart black homburg hat. Licking suddenly dry lips, I hoped the faded beige trousers I wore were not too filthy. At least I had remembered to take off my apron.

I raised a hand to return the greeting but couldn't resist touching my hair. I wished I'd dared dye it a bright and attention-grabbing blonde like Ruby's. Though the wide red headband I made from the sleeve of an old pullover mostly obscured my dull tresses.

Lizzie's tail thumped against my leg as the stranger crossed the street with long-legged strides. This had to be the new vicar, and my earlier statement to Lizzie that he was allegedly 'rather a dish', didn't quite cover it.

He had blue eyes fringed with dark eyelashes that curled upwards. Why was it that men's eyes always seemed to be so much prettier than women's? He was very tall and had a faint dusting of freckles across his nose and cheeks. I recalled that my gran had always referred to them as 'fairy kisses'. Swallowing the inappropriate need to share that information with him, I held out my hand.

'Martha Miller. Mrs. Pleased to meet you.'

I wished I hadn't made it so clear I was married. Realistically, though, trying to hide my marital status in this village was futile. He probably already knew exactly who I was. Maybe he had even intended to visit me to enquire after my husband and see if I needed him to pray for my forgiveness. Certainly, if Ada had spent any amount of time with the vicar since his arrival, she would have wasted no time in telling him all the latest theories.

He smiled, displaying a row of neat white teeth. This man was simply too good to be true. 'Mrs Martha Miller,' he repeated. 'How nice it is to meet you.'

'I live over there.' I pointed at my cottage.

But he most certainly would already know where I lived because, only moments earlier, I had closed my garden gate behind me and started up the lane. I was such a fool. Blaming my silly statement on my tiredness, I searched for a sensible and engaging topic.

Lizzie's tail swished from side to side, showing she was as excited to meet this handsome newcomer as I was. Fortunately for her, she was a dog and would not embarrass herself by saying something ridiculous simply to engage him in conversation. Bending his knees, the vicar enthusiastically stroked Lizzie's head with his large capable-looking hands. 'She's a beauty.'

'Yes.' I licked my lips again, wishing I was wearing anything but a blouse in muted lemon and trousers that once belonged to Stan. Although I had cut excess inches from the legs and hemmed them, there wasn't much I could do with the waistband. A piece of string currently held them up around my waist. I was certain that if I had on my best frock, and maybe a little of Ruby's lipstick, I would feel much more confident and conversation would flow easily between us. Sadly, I was just me. 'So, you're the new vicar, then?'

As if that wasn't obvious from the white collar around his neck. I was worse than a fool. I was a bumbling idiot. No wonder Stan had left me.

'Luke Walker.' He smiled again, and I wasn't sure whether he was being friendly or laughing at my social ineptitude. 'And, yes, I am the new vicar.'

'Is there a Mrs Walker?' I asked, peering over his shoulder as though his wife may be hiding behind Arthur Peters' hedge, waiting to spring up and introduce herself as soon as I asked after her.

'Unfortunately, I have yet to find someone willing to put up with me,' he said smoothly.

I found that very hard to believe but stopped myself from sharing that conviction with him. Looking down at my feet, I prepared myself for the inevitable question. Now I had asked about his spouse, he was likely to ask about mine. Unless, of course, Ada had already filled him in as I feared.

'Lizzie,' I blurted.

My cheeks burned as he looked at me in confusion. 'I thought you said your name was Martha?'

'Yes.' I nodded, then swallowed, embarrassment flooding through me. 'That is... My name is, indeed, Martha. My dog, who you were admiring, is called Lizzie.'

My garden gate banged shut and heels tapped on the pavement as Ruby walked quickly towards us. She wore a dress the exact shade of yellow as the peppers I'd harvested that morning. Her lips were painted bright red, her legs encased in sheer stockings, and her feet clad in a pair of black shoes I would have no hope of walking two steps in without falling flat on my face.

'Hullo,' she said coolly to Luke. 'I'm Ruby Andrews, Martha's younger sister.'

For one moment, anger flooded through me. Ruby had neatly styled hair, a pretty dress and ladylike shoes. I had none of those things. She'd also announced that I was the older sister. I suppressed a sigh. It was pointless being cross about a fact that was so patently obvious.

'I'll leave you two to talk,' I said hurriedly. 'I really should get on with walking Lizzie. It was nice to meet you, Vicar. Have a good evening, Ruby.'

I rushed away before either of them could respond.

Why on earth had I spent so much time wishing I had more human contact? The moment I had what I supposedly wanted, I had made myself look absurd by being unable to string together even the simplest of sentences.

* * *

'Obviously, he's very attractive,' I said to Lizzie when we returned home from our walk. 'But it's something more than that.'

I filled the kettle and put it onto the boiling plate on top of the Aga. Next, I opened my tea ball and measured out four teaspoons of lavender buds into it. Putting it in the teapot, I turned back to Lizzie. I don't suppose she cared very much, but I always thought it rather rude to talk to her while my back was turned.

'It seemed impossible for me to say anything that was even slightly intelligent,' I complained. 'He rendered me quite stupid.'

Lizzie tilted her head on one side and gave a wonderful impression of complete sympathy for my predicament.

'I expect church will be full on Sunday. This new fellow may well have the ability to charm even the cantankerous old biddies.' I bit my lip. 'I know it's desperately selfish of me, and none of my business, but I do hope he doesn't fall in love with Ruby.'

Lizzie didn't seem to care I wasn't being very loyal to my sister. I should have wanted a nice, decent chap like the new vicar to be interested in Ruby.

The kettle boiled, and I poured water into the teapot. While the tea stewed, I walked into the hallway and looked at myself critically in the oval-shaped mirror. I turned my head one way and then the other. It didn't alter my reflection, and neither did it tell me anything new.

'My nose is too pointed,' I told Lizzie as I went back into the kitchen. 'My hair is dull, and my clothes are old and shabby. For goodness' sake, I'm even wearing Stan's old trousers.'

I shook my head in self-disgust. It didn't matter what impression I had made on the vicar. Like it or not, I was married. Until such time as Stan came home, or the police found his body, there wasn't much I could do to change that fact.

Neither was it worth wasting my time feeling sorry for myself. I had long ago accepted my lot in this world. My marriage had been mostly unsatisfactory and, dare I say it, boring. I envied Ruby, who still had her life to live and choices I had not had before the war. Things were altering for women now. The world outside was changing – well, maybe for Ruby.

'But it's not any different for us though, is it, Lizzie?' I knelt before my faithful companion and rested one cheek against the side of her head. 'Nothing ever changes in Westleham.' Though that wasn't quite right. In the village, right now, someone was visiting gardens and destroying plants during the night. I shivered as I thought of someone doing that to my beloved crops. I wasn't like most of the other villagers, who gardened as a hobby or to enter something into the village show. Ruby and I depended on the food I grew.

'Right!' I got to my feet and poured myself a cup of lavender tea. 'I have felt sorry for myself for quite long enough. As mother would say, "There's no use crying over spilt milk." Let's go sit in the parlour.'

I turned on the wireless before sitting in my usual chair. There tended to be a play airing on a Friday evening, followed by a concert. Sometimes I would read or knit, but that night I felt too out of sorts to do anything but sit and sip my tea.

I hoped I would feel more like my usual self the next day. The village show was the biggest event in the village calendar, and as I was now deputy chair of the committee, there would be many demands on my time.

Remembering that Ruby had promised to lend me a dress for the occasion brightened my spirits, and I resolved to think less about handsome vicars that were beyond my reach and more about the positives in my life.

2

'I feel decidedly odd,' I said to Ruby. 'Not at all like myself.'

'Isn't that the point?' she said as she looked at me, her head tilted to one side. 'For one day, don't you think you deserve to look as much like a film star as I can manage?'

I frowned and looked back into the hall mirror. 'This pink lipstick is very flashy.'

Ruby shrugged. 'It's all the rage. All the girls are wearing it.'

I refrained from pointing out that it had been years since I was a girl. Turning my head to the side, I looked at my reflection again. The fuchsia colour painted on my lips was much bolder than any I would've chosen, while the hairstyle Ruby fashioned was far fancier than anything I could've managed myself. Add in the stylish dress and high-heeled shoes Ruby insisted I borrow, and my appearance was completely transformed. Well, except...

'My nose is still too pointy.'

'I can't do anything with that, you silly old thing.'

'No,' I agreed. 'I don't suppose anyone can.'

'Do you at least like your hair?'

I turned away from the mirror and looked at Ruby. 'You have worked absolute miracles. Thank you so much for everything you have done.'

Other sisters would have embraced, but that was not the way our parents raised us. I regretted the lack of emotional warmth they instilled in us more with every passing year. I showed more love towards Lizzie than I did my own sister.

Why was that?

'I saw Rita Hayworth in a magazine with her hair just like that,' Ruby said as she eyed me critically.

My clever sister had given me orders for what to do with my hair before I went to bed the previous evening. Dutifully, I contorted my arms to make sure the rollers Ruby had left on the dressing table in my room encased every strand of my hair in the exact way she instructed. I had to admit that my efforts were worth the temporary pain in my shoulders when I saw Ruby's work.

An hour ago, she removed the rollers and lifted my hair from the nape of my neck and fastened it on top of my head. She lightly backcombed the front, and the curls rested on top of this slight crest. Ruby drew the sides back smoothly, and fastened them, giving the entire hairdo a simple, elegant look. It also created the illusion that I had masses of hair instead of the thin, limp strands I usually hid under a headscarf.

In my borrowed dress, with my new hairstyle, I didn't look a bit like Martha Miller from Tulip Cottage, wife of Stan and keen gardener. I looked as though I might be off to London to see a show with a young man. Closing my eyes, I imagined my date holding out his hand to help me off the bus when we arrived at the West End. When the new vicar's face smiled back at me, I snapped out of my daydream. I had no business thinking of other men – but particularly one of Luke Walker's profession.

'I suppose we should leave.' A glance at the grandfather clock in the corner of the hall showed it was nine o'clock. The village fete wasn't due to start until eleven, but in my position as deputy chairwoman of the committee, there was an expectation that I arrive early and assist the chairwoman, Alice Warren, with any last-minute preparations.

'*You* should leave.' Ruby smiled and gave me a gentle push towards the front door. 'I shall be along later to lend moral support.'

'What if I fall flat on my face?'

'If you're going to fall, Martha, you will do that whether or not I am walking by your side.' Ruby opened the front door and watched me until I crossed the threshold. 'Don't forget what I told you. Keep your head up, your shoulders back and you will be fine.'

'You walk in shoes like this every weekend?' I frowned and looked down at the pretty shoes doubtfully. 'Perhaps I should have practised walking in them. I should probably come back inside and change into something more suitable.'

'They make your legs look very long and slim, which is the entire point.' Ruby made flapping motions with her hands. 'Now, off you go. You're worse than a child on the first day of school.'

Clutching my handbag closer to my body with one shaking hand, I took one step along the path before the door clicked softly closed behind me. There was no turning back now.

The laburnum tree to the right was in full bloom, its yellow flowers hanging down from slim branches. Little wonder it was known as 'golden rain'. I noticed several pods on the grass underneath the tree and contemplated rushing back indoors and tidying them up.

Had I told Ruby recently that they were poisonous, and Lizzie must not go near them? I couldn't remember.

Looking back at the house, I caught sight of Ruby in the front parlour. She had parted the net curtains and was pointing towards the gate at the end of the path. 'Go,' she mouthed.

Realistically, if Lizzie needed to go out, Ruby would let her out into the back garden, but it really shouldn't be necessary. I smiled to myself as I recalled furtively walking Lizzie early that morning, a headscarf covering the rollers I dare not touch and one of Stan's overcoats hiding the pyjamas I was frightened to take off in case I dislodged one of the pins holding the rollers in place.

What a fright I must have looked! Fortunately, I didn't see anyone as Lizzie and I walked away from the village towards Farmer Bennington's fields.

Reaching the garden gate, I hung on to it for a moment to fortify myself for the short walk to the village green where the show was to take place. Wishing I had an arm to hold to help keep my balance, I tottered down the lane.

My life would have probably been a lot easier if I'd stopped wishing for things I didn't have. Would Stan have offered an arm to me if he were there that morning? Not likely. He wouldn't have outright forbidden me from wearing high heels, bright lipstick and the fancy borrowed dress, but he certainly would have suggested I wash my face and change into something more sensible before leaving the house.

Not for the first time, I was glad he hadn't come home that day, but then the brief twinge of guilt wiped the smile from my face. Would it be like this forever? Every time I enjoyed something, would I feel remorseful because I didn't know whether Stan was alive or dead? It didn't seem very fair that I had to suffer because my husband had run off with some other woman.

Of course, I didn't know that's what he had done, but it seemed the likeliest scenario, although it would be extremely out of character. Stan was the sort of man who thrived on routine – he did everything in the exact same way, from preparing to leave the house for work, to what he did when he got home.

Every now and again, I allowed my mind to wonder about other possibilities. I quickly discounted him running off with the bank's daily takings and any other criminal activity – I would surely have been told if he were a fugitive. Neither could I imagine anyone harming him in any way. He was such an ordinary fellow.

Even the police thought he was involved with another woman and had left me to be with her. Once they had reassured themselves that Stan wasn't underneath my potato patch.

I closed the garden gate behind me, careful not to snag the brand-new stockings Ruby had given me, and followed her advice.

Head up, shoulders back, I looked down the lane that led into the centre of Westleham and started walking.

* * *

It was soon eleven o'clock and villagers streamed from their homes and onto the green. The sun blazed down onto trestle tables covered with cloths as white as the clouds that bobbed across the blue sky.

'It's going to be a wonderful turnout, Mrs Miller,' Alice Warren called to me as she sailed past with a clipboard in one hand, a pen in the other.

'All down to your wonderful planning,' I said to her retreating back.

The annual village show was taking place for the first time since before war had broken out in Europe. As soon as the date was announced, excitement had spread quickly throughout the village. It was the first celebration since VE Day and was very eagerly anticipated.

'I'm surprised anyone has bothered turning up.' Ada Garrett stopped inside the small marquee erected by some of the village men. Later, it would be where the winners of each of the show categories were announced. Trust Ada to try to put a dampener on the day that not even the English weather was attempting to spoil.

I stacked a few more glasses onto the table from the box sent over by the Cricketer's Arms, the village pub, for us to use that day. It gave me the time I needed to form a polite response to the cantankerous old gossip. 'It's the first village show for years, Mrs Garrett. I should think the entire village will be here.'

'Much of the village has nothing to enter into the show.' Her gaze raked over me from the curls on top of my head to the tips of Ruby's shoes that were now pinching my toes very uncomfortably.

'I'm very sorry that has happened,' I said placatingly. The woman was infuriating. The damage caused to villagers' gardens was a terrible act of vandalism, but it had nothing to do with me.

'Are you really?' Ada put a hand on an ample hip and eyed me with blatant dislike.

Someone really ought to tell Ada Garrett that when she tilted her head at that exact angle, it made the hairs growing from the mole on the side of her face so much more obvious. That person would not be me.

I raised an eyebrow. 'Why wouldn't I be sorry?'

She gave me another slow once over. 'Look at you, done up like a dog's dinner. You obviously expect to win every prize on offer.'

'On the contrary, Mrs Garrett,' I said pleasantly – I was accustomed to Ada's acidic tone and forthright manner of speech. It was so much easier to be nice to the woman when staring directly at her hairy mole rather than her pinched face and angry eyes.

'Oh, come now, Mrs Miller. Yours is one of the few gardens not damaged. Your garden produce is the talk of the village.'

That was nice to hear. At least they weren't talking about Stan and where I'd buried him any more.

'I'm flattered that people think the food I grow in my garden is of a good standard.'

'I expect that's because it has good fertiliser,' Ada snapped back, obviously frustrated her words were not causing me to react in the way she wanted. 'Your poor husband.'

Digging into the handbag resting on the side of the table, I pulled out a handkerchief and dabbed at the corners of my eyes, hoping she would feel remorseful enough to leave me alone. 'Yes. It's been a year today since my poor Stan went missing.'

'Your crocodile tears don't fool me.' Ada leaned forward. 'I *know* what you did to that unfortunate man.'

She was right about one thing – I couldn't cry proper tears for my missing husband, but I truly did not know where he was. Did the vicious old woman really think I enjoyed working such long hours in the garden simply so Ruby and I could eat? Although Ada habitually said whatever was on her mind, her words stung. I couldn't imagine what it was about me that made her think I was capable of killing my husband.

'What an unkind thing to say,' I replied, wanting nothing more than to suggest to her that she go home and attend to the hairs sprouting from her face.

'If you're dressed like that because you think the new vicar will look your way, you would do well to remember you're a married woman.'

'I'm dressed this way because I am the deputy chair of the

village committee and it's important I look professional.' I swallowed my hurt and spoke as grandly as I could. 'Though, honestly, I was rather hoping the vicar would give me a second look while I was all dressed up. Looking hurt no one, did it?'

'If you win a prize, Mrs Miller, the entire village will be in uproar.'

'I'm pleased I can reassure you then,' I said smoothly. 'I am positive I won't win a single prize this year.'

That stopped Ada in her tracks, though her mouth hung open like a fish on a hook. Eventually, she regained her composure and pointed a fat forefinger at me. 'I'm watching you.'

And I'm watching you to see how fast your mole hairs grow.

I opened my mouth to say the words on my mind but was saved from dropping down to Ada's level by the man who earlier featured in my fantasy West End date.

'Good morning, ladies.' Luke ducked his head as he walked through the entrance to the marquee. 'Hasn't the good Lord sent us a beautiful day?'

'He has indeed, Vicar,' I murmured.

'I understand you have the best garden in the village, Mrs Miller.'

'That's very nice to hear.'

'Only because hers hasn't been sabotaged.' Ada glared at me with such hate I took a step back. I didn't know what I had done to cause her to dislike me so much.

'I have been incredibly fortunate the vandal has not attacked my garden.' I forced myself to smile at the poisonous woman. 'Otherwise, I don't know how Ruby and I would manage during the winter without my garden produce to feed us.'

The vicar gave me an admiring glance while Ada turned an unbecoming shade of red. 'But surely I heard you correctly a moment ago? You suggested you won't win any prizes this year. How can that be if yours is the best garden?'

I smiled brightly at Ada before giving my full attention to Luke. 'I decided not to enter the show. As I'm on the committee, it didn't seem ethical.'

It wasn't a complete lie. Not entering the show had less to do with my morals and more to do with the fact that winning would not give me a monetary prize. I didn't need rosettes. I needed to feed my little family.

'How very noble,' Luke said admiringly. 'And may I say how fetching you look today in that dress.'

'You're too kind,' I mumbled quickly, finding it hard to fill my lungs with enough air to both breathe and speak.

He turned to Ada. 'What a marvellous hat! Such decorative feathers.'

'Why, thank you, Vicar.' Ada touched his arm. 'Perhaps you would let me show you where you can sample my gooseberry jam?'

'I would be delighted, Mrs Garrett.'

Ada threw me a triumphant look as she exited the marquee with the vicar, but completely missed the wink he sent my way.

What did that mean? Had he heard Ada's unkind words and come into the marquee to rescue me, or did it mean something else entirely?

It didn't matter because Ada was right. I wasn't a free woman, but it was nice to receive a little attention from a man. Stan had never looked at me in appreciation in his life – not even on the day we married.

Returning to my task of placing the borrowed glasses on the table, I resolved not to let my imagination run away with me. However much I enjoyed the vicar's kindness, we could never be more than friends.

It would probably take my wildly galloping heart a little while to calm down long enough to hear the sensible message my brain was trying to send around my overexcited body – he was the village vicar, and I was a married woman.

* * *

Later that afternoon, the judges completed their tasks. Flowers had been examined, vegetables admired, jam sampled. As was usual in small village shows, the judges were local bigwigs. In Westleham's case, that meant the Earl of Chesden, who lived in a manor house beyond Farmer Bennington's fields, and the local member of parliament, Rupert Gosford. If they were not in agreement, Lady Chesden's opinion was sought. Alice informed me with an air of authority that Lady Chesden had never disagreed with her husband's choice in all the years the show had taken place.

'Shall we begin?' Alice trilled excitedly.

Florence Noble, the publican's daughter, moved among the villagers with a tray, making sure everyone had a glass of my plum gin before Alice made the announcements.

Children played outside the marquee and somewhere a dog barked. Towards the back of the crowd, I could see Ruby. She took a sip of her drink and raised it in my direction. Tradition dictated that the chairperson drank first, everyone else followed with a toast, and the chair then announced the prizes. I wish I cared as much for conventions as my sister.

'First, a toast.' Alice raised her glass. 'This year, Westleham Village Committee is pleased to enjoy the delightful plum gin provided by our very own Mrs Miller. I'm sure you will all join me in thanking Mrs Miller for her generosity.'

I nodded and smiled at the murmurs of thanks that rippled through the audience. It was true I had donated several bottles of gin to the committee for their use during the village show, but only because I hoped it would prove so popular villagers would pay for it in the future. Joe Noble, the publican, had secured a deal with the brewery to sell my gin in his pub.

It had been a long time since I last did something simply to be kind. Sadly, since Stan's disappearance, my actions were usually motivated by whatever was in it for me.

Alice held the glass close to her mouth. 'Lord and Lady Chesden, and Mr Gosford, our esteemed guests. To Westleham, to our village show, our committee, and our wonderful villagers!'

Alice drank, and everyone else followed suit. For a long moment, the mood of euphoric celebration lingered.

Then Alice staggered forward. She crashed into the table in front of her, sending plants and jars tumbling to the floor. Someone shrieked, followed by the high-pitched racket of glasses smashing as Florence dropped the tray of plum gin. Her eyes wide, she stared at Alice in horror.

Galvanised into action by the distress in Florence's eyes, I reached over to take hold of Alice. Her hands grasped her neck as though trying to claw the liquid she'd consumed out of her throat. She was too heavy for me to hold upright, and together we slumped to the floor. Alice desperately gasped for breath.

Someone called for Doctor Briggs. A man's frantic voice called out the name, 'Alice'. Women screamed. Chaos reigned.

Was she having some sort of fit? I had no medical training whatsoever. I didn't know what to do. Never before had I felt more inadequate or ill prepared. Holding Alice's head in my lap, I smoothed her hair back from her forehead with shaking fingers in the same way I'd seen mothers do with their children.

As Doctor Briggs forced his way through the crowd and crouched next to me, Alice's body stilled. Less than two minutes had passed since her exuberant toast, but it seemed that was quite long enough.

Alice Warren was dead.

3

'Come along, Mrs Miller, let's get you up off the floor.' Luke held out a hand to me, then leaned forward and peered at me closely. 'Are you feeling unwell?'

Shaking my head, I reached out my fingers to meet his. They were shaking like leaves in the autumn wind. 'I'm fine.'

My voice sounded high and strained, nothing like my usual tone. He hauled me to my feet. I looked at the grass next to our feet where Alice lay. Doctor Briggs hunched over her, performing artificial respiration. Even without the benefit of medical training, I knew it was pointless. No one could survive their face turning that ghastly shade of purple.

'My plum gin,' I whispered as I looked back to Luke, the colour of Alice's face reminding me that the last thing she consumed was poured from the bottles of alcohol that I made. My stomach lurched at the possibility that my plum gin could have had something to do with Alice's death.

'I drank my entire glass,' he said. 'I'm fine.'

He had a very comforting manner about him. I expect they taught vicars that at the seminary. They all had that similar way about them – like there was nothing the world could throw their way that would fluster them.

'My darling!' Charles, Alice's husband, hurried over to his wife's prone figure. 'Please wake up, my sweet.'

'Are you sure you feel all right?' Luke looked at me, then at Charles.

'Of course.' I nodded vigorously. 'You must tend to Charles.'

My neck ached from my zealous affirmation, as though it wasn't quite strong enough to hold my head upright. I wanted nothing more than to go home and lie in bed with a warm quilt covering my entire body.

'Martha, my goodness. What happened?' Ruby reached my side and put an arm around me.

I was so grateful for her presence and support that I promptly burst into tears. 'It was awful, Ruby, just dreadful.'

'Is she dead?' she whispered, leading me over to the side of the marquee and away from Alice's body.

'Most certainly,' I told her, looking around for my handbag. 'I need a hankie.'

Ruby plucked one out of her bag and handed it over. 'Here. You poor old thing.'

'I'll ruin it.'

'You do all the washing, Martha, so do your worst.'

I mopped the tears from my face and blew my nose. Ruby squeezed my shoulder. 'I can't believe Mrs Warren just collapsed and died right in front of the entire village.'

'And after drinking your plum gin too.'

'Ruby!' I admonished. 'What a thing to say.'

'I didn't mean there was anything wrong with your gin.'

I shrugged off her comforting arm. 'Then why say such a thing?'

'I only meant—'

'I know what you meant.' I sighed. It wasn't Ruby's fault she had stated the obvious. No doubt the entire village would arrive at the same conclusion – if they hadn't already. 'Ada has already been beastly enough to me today without this.'

'Ada is a nasty old witch.' Ruby looked over her shoulder, as though to check the older woman wasn't within earshot. 'This is probably her fault. I expect she put a spell on Mrs Warren.'

'I don't think I believe in witchcraft.' Smiling quickly at Ruby to show there were no hard feelings for her words, I crumpled the soiled handkerchief in my hand. I wished I hadn't been so quick to move away from her embrace. It was nice to feel as though I wasn't completely alone. 'Thank you, Ruby.'

She frowned, confusion sitting in lines across her forehead. 'What for?'

I grabbed one of her hands. 'For being here with me.'

'I must question you immediately, Mrs Miller.' PC Cyril Bottomley, the village policeman, looked between Ruby and me. His expression suggested he held us entirely responsible for Alice's fate. 'Don't go anywhere, Miss Andrews. I shall need to speak to you, too.'

'I will be straight back when I have got a chair for my sister,' Ruby retorted. 'Any fool can see that she is in shock. Her legs are shaking more than Mrs Garrett's third chin.'

I hid a smile at Ruby's impolite words and, not for the first time, wished I felt comfortable expressing my thoughts as easily as she did. Maybe it was because she worked in a factory with lots of other young women and it gave her the confidence to say what she thought instead of measuring her words as I did.

Ruby quickly returned with a chair, and I sank gratefully onto it. Cyril glared at Ruby. Whether it was because he expected her to bring him a seat, or because he was waiting for her to leave, I wasn't sure, but she stationed herself next to me and returned his stare with one of her own.

I couldn't remember a time when I had been prouder of my baby sister.

'Mrs Miller, can you tell me what happened?'

I cleared my throat, and forced myself not to fidget, before I spoke as clearly as I could, despite my frazzled nerves. 'Alice was about to announce the winners of the show. She made a toast, drank some of her plum gin and collapsed.'

'Plum gin I believe you are responsible for making?'

My heart seemed to skip a beat, leaving me slightly breathless. Cyril had quickly reached the same conclusion that I had. The last thing Alice had drunk before her collapse was my gin. I was certain there was nothing wrong with it, and no one else appeared to have suffered any ill effects, but that didn't stop an overwhelming guilt threatening to suffocate me. 'That is correct.'

Cyril jerked his head in Alice's direction. 'It looks like a case of poisoning.'

'Surely not,' I said, even though that was the obvious conclusion. 'Perhaps she had some sort of health issue and that caused her collapse.'

'No one else is ill,' Ruby added. 'And I drank every single drop of my drink because Martha's plum gin is delicious.'

'Thank you, Miss Andrews.' Cyril raised an eyebrow in her direction. No gratitude showed on his florid face. 'Did everyone join in the toast?'

'Everyone that I could see,' she answered.

'Then someone has deliberately tried to kill Mrs Warren,' Cyril announced.

'They haven't *tried* to do anything.' I shuddered, remembering Alice's face. 'They succeeded. She's dead.'

'Indeed.' Cyril rocked back on his heels. His large moon-shaped face was red and sweaty, and he looked completely out of his depth.

'Anything else?' Ruby clipped. 'Because if there isn't, I'd like to get my sister home for a cup of hot sweet tea. She's had a terrible shock.'

Hastily, Cyril removed his notebook from a pocket on his too-tight uniform. He licked the end of his pencil before laboriously scratching some words onto a page. 'Did you bring the bottles of gin with you this morning?'

I hoped my face did not betray my surprise. That was actually an intelligent question. 'I did not. I delivered them to the pub earlier this week.'

He wrote something else before snapping his notebook closed. 'I think I need to speak to Joe.'

Joe Noble was the owner of the village pub, the Cricketer's Arms, and the father of Florence, who had acted as a waitress in the marquee.

'Don't you think you might need to telephone for reinforcements?' Ruby suggested.

'What do you mean by that?' Cyril's voice rose and a bead of sweat rolled down his face.

'If Mrs Warren has been killed,' Ruby kept her voice low, 'then you will surely need help. There are far too many villagers for just you to interview.'

'And you spend a lot of time in the Cricketer's Arms,' I said, eyeing the tight waistband of Cyril's uniform.

'What are you suggesting?' Cyril pulled a handkerchief that was more grey than white from his pocket and swiped it across his face.

'Only that I understand investigations should be unbiased.' I repeated the line one of the policemen looking into Stan's disappearance had said to me last year. That was apparently the reason they sent detectives from Scotland Yard to speak to me. 'As you live in the village, and frequently drink in the local pub—'

'Perhaps I should rule myself out of the investigation.' Cyril looked thoughtful. 'I will telephone to Slough for advice.'

As he left, I let out a long breath of relief. 'I thought he was going to arrest me.'

Ruby shook her head in disgust. 'He has made no progress identifying whoever it is vandalising village gardens – I wouldn't trust his ability to find a killer.'

'The life of a village policeman suits Cyril,' I agreed. 'So long as the crimes remain relatively unimportant. Murder is too much for him.'

Whilst I was glad Ruby's thoughts matched my own, they were of little comfort. We lived in a small Berkshire village, not in the middle of London. Wanton vandalism and murder were crimes I never thought would happen in our quiet spot of England. I had always felt safe in Westleham. That comfort had been snatched away in the most wicked of circumstances. How could any of us rest easily now it seemed there was not only a vandal but a killer loose in the village?

Who on earth would want to kill Alice Warren? And why?

* * *

My attention was caught by a wail of anguish that erupted from Charles Warren. Like a swollen river bursting its banks, his emotions were clearly too fierce to be kept inside. 'No, no, no!'

Fresh tears ran down my cheeks at his naked grief. I had never seen the man show any excessive feelings before. Until now, he'd reminded me rather of Stan, though my husband was a good deal shorter. But they shared the same look of importance and self-containment. Neither smiled very often nor showed any signs of dismay. Except for now, of course. Charles Warren looked, and sounded, absolutely broken.

'Poor man,' Ruby murmured. 'Who would've thought that he loved Alice quite that much?'

I tried to visualise Stan showing such pain if it were me lying on the grass dead, but the only thing I could imagine him to be upset about was that he would have to make his own meals and do his own washing. Though that was perhaps a little unfair, because my own overriding concern when Stan had gone missing was how I would pay the bills. It was only later I worried about his well-being. Every now and again, I looked at the single bed next to mine in the room we shared and felt a little melancholy, but there had been no outpouring of distress like Charles was exhibiting. What did that say about me as a person, and a wife?

'Reminds me a little of Reverend Gibbs,' I said, recalling when the old vicar had sagged to the church floor in the middle of his sermon. 'So dramatic and unexpected.'

'I thought he died of a heart attack,' Ruby said, confusion etched across her face. 'You don't think there are any similarities?'

'Perhaps Alice had a heart attack too.' I shrugged. 'It's possible.'

Ruby didn't disagree with me, but I could see that she thought it was very unlikely Alice's death was natural. 'Stay here, I shall go fetch you a cup of tea.'

I wasn't sure where else Ruby thought I would go. I didn't trust my legs to carry me back to the house, and it seemed rude somehow to walk out of the marquee and leave Alice just lying there.

Someone brought over a white sheet and settled it over Alice's prone figure. I looked away, but it didn't help. I could still recall how her face twisted grotesquely as she struggled for breath. Doctor Briggs helped Charles to his feet. Sobbing uncontrollably, he allowed the doctor to lead him out of the marquee.

'The doctor thinks he needs to be sedated,' Luke said. I hadn't even heard him come over. 'For the shock.'

'Ruby is bringing a cup of tea to help with mine,' I said, then immediately wished I had stayed quiet. Charles Warren had lost his wife. My shock wasn't remotely comparable.

'A fine idea.' Luke tapped his fingers on the back of my chair. 'You have very little colour in your face, Mrs Miller.'

The only reason my complexion wasn't generally as washed out and faded as the rest of me was because of the warm weather we had experienced lately and the fact I spent most of the day outside in the garden. I hated to think what the bouts of crying had done to my face and the make-up Ruby had carefully applied. No doubt I looked terrible.

Not that it mattered. Luke was the vicar, and I was one of his parishioners.

Perhaps if I had thought of him as simply 'the vicar', as opposed to his Christian name, it would have reminded me that he was about as off limits to me as women were to Catholic priests.

'Is the doctor taking Mr Warren home?'

'Yes. The doctor's wife will sit with him while the doctor comes back here to wait for the police.' For the first time in our brief acquaintance, the vicar looked unsure. 'He asked me to stay here.'

'In the marquee?'

'With the body,' he clarified. 'He said the police would want her to remain in situ.'

'I see.' I didn't, not really. My only experience with the police had been after Stan's disappearance. Surely they were treating

Alice's death as seriously as they would a murder? 'I suppose the doctor wants to make sure I don't touch anything.'

He frowned. 'Why would you say that?'

'It was my plum gin,' I repeated my earlier words to him. 'You don't know this village yet. Though surely you have been here long enough to have heard the gossip about me burying my husband under my potatoes?'

He grinned, then realised I was serious. 'I hadn't heard that.'

'I'm surprised.'

'He isn't, is he?'

I looked at him sharply. He lifted one corner of his mouth in a half-smile to show he was joking. It probably wasn't right to share a moment of levity in the circumstances, but it was nice to have a brief instance of normality. 'No, he isn't. I promise.'

'I believe you.'

'Just like that?'

'Yes, you have an honest face, Mrs Miller.'

I didn't care if his reason was superficial. It felt so lovely to have a person other than Ruby believe in me. Especially one who was showing he was as kind as he was handsome. 'You surely don't believe you can tell if a person is honest simply by looking at their face?'

'I am very good at spotting a liar.' His words were rather boastful, but they didn't sound so coming from him.

Ruby handed me a hideous green teacup and matching saucer. It was without a doubt the ugliest crockery I had ever seen. 'Oh, Ruby, you are a darling. Thank you.'

'Would you like a cup of tea, Vicar?' Ruby asked.

Luke put a hand in his pocket, drew out a few coins and handed them over to Ruby. 'I would appreciate it very much if you would get me a cup of tea, Miss Andrews. I'm afraid the doctor has insisted I stay here in the marquee, otherwise I would suggest you stay with your sister while I fetch my own refreshments.'

Ruby looked down at the money he had placed in her hand. 'How many cups of tea do you want? You've given me enough to cover tea for half the village.'

Luke leaned forward as though he were about to impart a great secret. 'My housekeeper's cooking leaves a lot to be desired. If it wouldn't trouble you too greatly, perhaps you could pick up some sandwiches? And maybe some biscuits too.'

'Mrs Jennings makes the most gorgeous Victoria sponge cake. She uses her own strawberry jam in the filling. Shall I get you a slice if there's any left?'

'Two slices would be champion.'

Ruby giggled. 'Vicar, do you have a sweet tooth?'

'I'm afraid that I do,' he admitted. 'Now, do you have enough money for all of that?'

'I'm certain there will be change.'

Ruby hurried off to the stalls on the green outside the marquee, and Luke turned back to face me. 'Hopefully, I can encourage you to share in a spot of lunch when your sister returns?'

'I don't think I could eat a thing.' I put a hand on my stomach. 'Just the thought of food makes me feel quite queasy. Poor Mrs Warren.'

'Drink your tea,' he instructed. 'If your colour returns, I promise not to natter at you any more about eating. If it does not, I will insist you have something.'

I nodded as obediently as a child to its mother. It was very pleasant to have someone worry about my welfare, even if he was only doing so because it was his job. A vicar had a duty to care for all his parishioners – even those that were likely to be arrested the moment the real police arrived from Slough.

* * *

'There she is!' Startled by the sudden harshness of the woman's voice, tea sloshed from the cup into the saucer. I stared at the over-stewed liquid for a moment before looking up to see Elsie Harrington marching towards me in her sensible shoes. 'I hope you don't think the death of Mrs Warren means you will be the new chairwoman of the village committee.'

I stopped myself from pointing out that the rules of the West-leham Village Committee allowed for the exact scenario Mrs Harrington now sought to prevent. It was typical of Elsie to insert herself into the most shocking event in Westleham since the previous vicar had dropped down dead after delivering his sermon, so I didn't take her words personally. Looking pointedly towards the cloth-covered body of the former chairwoman, I met her harsh stare calmly. 'To be honest, Mrs Harrington, I feel rather uncomfortable discussing such matters right now.'

'It is pointless pretending you are better than you are,' she hissed.

Luke moved away from my side and rested a hand on Mrs Harrington's arm. 'I think perhaps we should all allow what has happened to sink in and regain control of our normal emotions.'

'I am in full control of my emotions, thank you, Vicar,' Elsie snapped. 'That woman is a menace to this village.'

I was wrong. This was an entirely personal attack. I couldn't imagine what I'd done to make her so venomous. 'I don't feel this is the right time—'

'It is entirely the correct time to speak my mind,' she retorted and pointed at me. Her finger was only millimetres away from the end of my nose. 'You must understand that we will not tolerate your machinations in this village.'

'Machinations?' Luke repeated in a bewildered voice.

'You are too new to the village to be fully aware of her deceit.' Elsie didn't look at Luke but carried on glaring at me as though I were some modern-day version of Mary Ann Cotton. Tears of humiliation pricked at the back of my eyes as I stared resolutely at the ground.

'So far as I am aware, Mrs Miller has not been charged with any crime,' Luke replied calmly. It took every bit of my self-discipline to keep my gaze on Elsie's ugly shoes and not smile in gratitude at Luke.

'I'm sad to see that you have allowed yourself to be dragged into her web, Vicar.' Elsie shook her head as though she had received particularly devastating news. 'Let us hope you don't pay with your life in the same way as the last man whom she ensnared.'

I wanted to laugh. It was all so fantastical. Elsie wouldn't listen to the truth, but I longed to tell her I hadn't done a single thing to catch Stan. We had met at a distant cousin's wedding. He was single, and I was single. War had just broken out in Europe and the uncertainty of the world made us both desperate to cling to a bit of normality.

I certainly hadn't charmed Stan with my stunning good looks, sparkling personality or child-bearing hips. It no longer pained me to admit that I was rather plain, extremely dull to most people, and my figure was more like that of a young boy than a woman built for effortlessly giving her husband as many children as he may require.

Elsie Harrington, on the other hand, was what most people would imagine when thinking of the perfect business owner's wife. She had a pleasant face – when she wasn't spouting vitriol in my direction, of course. Which was odd, now I came to think of it. I'd never seen her act this way before. Elsie was also extremely good at organising and taking part in good works. She volunteered on every committee in a fifty-mile radius of Westleham. To top it all off, she had a perfect family of two boys and two girls. In short, she was precisely what I wasn't.

Ruby hurried back into the marquee laden down with a tray. 'Here we are, Vicar.'

'You are an angel. Thank you so much, Miss Andrews.'

Elsie looked at me and Luke, then behind her at Ruby. 'It's like that, is it?'

Luke's hand, halfway to grabbing a sandwich, dropped back to his side. 'I'm terribly sorry, Mrs Harrington, but you've lost me.'

'Mixing yourself up with these... *trollops* is a dreadful move on your part. The bishop will hear of this, you can mark my words.'

'What is going on?' Ernest Harrington arrived and put an arm around his wife's shoulder. 'You appear quite overwrought, my dear.'

'Oh, you wouldn't understand, *you're* as bad as *he* is.'

'Darling,' he tried again. 'What has caused you such distress?'

'That woman' – Elsie pointed at me again – 'has poisoned Alice. And now she's got her claws into the vicar. He'll be dead next. Just like her husband, and poor Alice.'

I opened my mouth to refute Elsie's wicked accusations. The last thing I needed was for the few people who thought I hadn't killed my husband to think there was some truth in Elsie's words. It was difficult enough to command respect as a 'single' woman in an old-fashioned village without people believing I had done something to bring about my status.

I didn't dare look at the vicar to see how he had reacted to Elsie's tirade. Over the last hour or so, I had come to believe that he could become a friend and goodness knew how few of those I had in the village. I hated to think that Elsie and her mad claims might put paid to that friendship before it had even begun to blossom.

'I do apologise,' Ernest said smoothly. 'My wife has not been well lately. Please excuse us.'

Elsie stared at me for a long moment. 'Ernest, you must *do* something!'

'Come along, dear,' he replied in a voice that adults usually reserve for explaining things to very young children.

Elsie sobbed loudly as her husband led her out of the marquee.

Ruby placed the tray on the grass next to my chair and lifted the plate filled with sandwiches. 'Hurry, Vicar. You had better eat something now before the next village lunatic arrives to ruin your appetite.'

'Ruby,' I admonished. 'That's not very kind.'

'Perhaps not,' she agreed. 'But it's truth. The woman has clearly taken leave of her senses. She's talking complete nonsense.'

I couldn't really disagree with Ruby's assessment, but Elsie's behaviour was completely out of character. Normally, she was a very level-headed woman. Something was very wrong in the village of Westleham and it seemed that I was caught right in the middle of it.

4

'Ah, Mrs Miller, here you are.' Margaret Leaming walked purposefully towards me, and I braced myself for more insults. Luke looked at his fish-paste sandwich sorrowfully. It seemed he would remain hungry if he intended to stay by my side and protect me from those in the village who wished to malign my character.

'Mrs Leaming.' My greeting sounded forced, even to my own ears.

She folded her arms across her tweed suit, which was surely too warm for the beautiful summer weather. Her action stressed her ample bosom and, at the same time, made her look like a strict Victorian governess.

'You poor thing. You must have been terrified.'

Surprised, my gaze snapped up to meet Margaret's concern-filled blue eyes. 'I was expecting you to tell me how this is all my fault.'

'Goodness, why would I say such a thing?'

'Everyone else is,' I said morosely. It was a slight exaggeration. Only Elsie had openly accused me, but I wasn't stupid. I could see that every time someone stood in the opening of the marquee and looked my way that they were thinking exactly the same as Elsie. It was written all over their faces and glowed in their accusatory glares.

'Everyone?' Margaret raised an eyebrow. 'Surely not?'

'Sandwich, Mrs Leaming?' Ruby lifted the plate and offered it to the committee secretary. 'Or perhaps you'd rather a slice of cake?'

'I'm jolly keen on cake,' Margaret confirmed. 'Is it Mrs Jennings's Victoria sponge? I can only dream of making a cake as light as hers.'

'Do help yourself.' Ruby lifted the other plate from the tray and passed Mrs Leaming a napkin.

Margaret took a bite of cake and made a sound of pure delight. 'Goodness, this is first rate.'

I couldn't help but admire Margaret. With a mouth so full of cake, I wouldn't have been able to utter one word, let alone a coherent sentence. She had also gone out of her way to find me and be friendly, which I very much appreciated. We had spoken many times at committee meetings and if we saw each other in the village, but we'd never been great friends. That she would make such an effort to seek me out made me hope that not everyone thought as badly of me as Ada and Elsie.

'You don't think my sister poisoned Mrs Warren, then?' Ruby enquired.

'I saw your sister drinking the plum gin,' Margaret said before cramming the last bit of cake into her mouth. She dabbed at her mouth with the napkin in a very ladylike way – which was in direct odds to how she'd eaten the cake. She swallowed the last bit of cake. 'Why would Mrs Miller put poison in the gin then drink it herself?'

'That is precisely what I said,' Luke said.

'Thank goodness you have the common sense you were born with, Vicar.' Margaret shook her head. 'It seems some in this village left theirs behind in their cradle.'

'Assuming they had some in the first place,' Ruby commented wryly.

'Indeed.' Margaret looked admiringly at Ruby. 'What a sensible young woman you are. Before today, I assumed you were all red lipstick and empty head.'

'I'm very glad to hear you have changed your opinion of me.' Ruby laughed.

'The question, I suppose, is what are we to do about the way everyone else sees my sister?'

Three pairs of eyes looked my way. I sipped at my lukewarm tea to give myself a moment to think of how to respond. 'I'm not sure what I can do to alter people's belief about what happened.'

'You must do something!' Margaret said with gusto. 'It just won't do for you to go back to your cottage and carry on being the quiet little mouse you usually are. You must stand up for yourself, Mrs Miller.'

'Don't I always tell you that?' Ruby crowed. 'You shouldn't let people take advantage of you, Martha. You're much too nice.'

'Other than taking out an advertisement in the local paper to insist Stan isn't buried underneath my potatoes, I'm not sure what I can do. Folk around here believe what they want to believe.' Most villagers distrusted me after Stan's disappearance. It would only be worse now my gin was linked to Alice's death.

'Perhaps when they are due to be harvested, you should hold an event at your house,' Margaret suggested.

'An event? I don't follow.'

'Have everyone come around with a spade. They dig up the potatoes. If they find a dead body, they get to keep the potatoes and report you to the police. If they do not, they must hand over all the potatoes they have harvested to you.'

After the horror of seeing Alice die in front of me, Margaret's idea sounded like the funniest thing I'd heard in such a long time. The four of us laughed together until my sides complained.

'Oh, Mrs Leaming,' Ruby gasped between giggles. 'That is quite a magnificent plan.'

An incredibly handsome man in a suit walked into the marquee, followed by Cyril Bottomley, who pointed my way. 'That is Mrs Miller.'

I struggled to straighten my face into composed lines of sorrow. Or at least something that didn't make it look as though I was having a jolly good time with my friends whilst a woman lay dead not three metres away from us.

'Good day, Mrs Miller.' He lifted a black hat to reveal thick blond hair that curled over his collar. Clever green eyes looked over me, and my heart stopped. A moment before he opened his mouth to speak again, I knew exactly who he was. 'I am Detective Inspector Robertson. I'm here to investigate the suspicious death of Mrs Alice Warren.'

Of course he was.

* * *

'Perhaps we could speak somewhere a little more private?' Luke suggested.

The detective stared at Luke, paying particular attention to the white collar around his neck that proclaimed his profession. 'Are you Mr Miller?'

Luke coughed awkwardly. 'I am not. My name is Luke Walker. I am the vicar.'

'I see.' The detective looked from me to Luke, then to Ruby. 'And you are?'

'Ruby Andrews. I am Martha's sister. I live with her.'

'Very well. I will interview you and your sister in your home.' The detective turned to Cyril, who stood at his side, shuffling his feet while studiously avoiding looking in Alice's direction. 'You are to stay here with the vicar until the doctor returns. When he does, Vicar, I presume you will go home?'

'Yes.' Luke glanced in my direction. 'I will be at the vicarage.'

'Thank you, Vicar,' I said. 'You have been most kind.'

'All in a day's work,' he replied, then flushed. 'Apart from the murder, of course. That's not in anyone's usual workday.'

'Apart from mine,' the detective said dryly. His expression suggested he thought we were all bumbling village idiots. Which, unfortunately, was exactly how we were acting.

'I shall call and see you tomorrow,' Margaret said as I got to my feet. 'We can discuss outstanding committee business then.'

Although she had made me laugh moments earlier, which was a much needed release after the shock of watching Alice die, I wished Margaret hadn't come to find me. Now the detective would think we were all sitting around eating cake and talking about committee business while Alice lay dead nearby.

Was it possible for me to look any more guilty in his eyes?

Ruby and I walked down the lane together, with the detective following behind. I opened the door and Lizzie rushed to greet us. I dropped to one knee to embrace her. 'Hello, my darling. Did you miss me?'

'Lizzie is Martha's very best friend,' Ruby said by way of explanation.

'Show the detective into the parlour, Ruby,' I said. Kicking off my borrowed shoes and shoving my feet into my slippers, I tried desperately not to sigh with the relief of getting rid of the items of foot torture. 'I'll make a tea tray and bring it in.'

'I'll help,' Ruby said eagerly.

It wasn't a two-person job, and Ruby never usually offered to help in the kitchen, but I couldn't think of a way to rebuff her offer without us looking even more odd to the detective. I pointed at the closed door on the left of the narrow corridor. 'The parlour is through there. Please make yourself comfortable.'

Lizzie trotted after us into the kitchen. I shook the kettle to make sure there was enough water in it, then put it to boil on the stovetop. 'Why did you tell him Lizzie is my best friend?'

Ruby shrugged and slumped into one of the kitchen chairs. 'She is. And you made such a fuss of her, I felt like I had to do something to excuse your behaviour.'

'What was wrong with my behaviour?' I frowned as I grabbed the big tray and put it on the table.

'We were all laughing in the marquee, then you came home and got on the floor to greet your dog. The detective didn't see you weeping earlier, or your clear distress at what happened to the unfortunate Mrs Warren. I didn't want him to think you were cold and heartless and only capable of showing emotion to an animal.'

I blinked, momentarily stunned that anyone would think my greeting towards Lizzie was anything but normal. Slowly, Ruby's words hit their mark. 'Thank you.'

Was that how people saw me? Could that be why they were so eager to jump to the conclusion I was involved in Stan's disappearance? Perhaps if the villagers perceived me to be an unemotional woman whose only real friend was a dog, it was easier to believe bad things about me. I wanted to ask Ruby if that was how she saw me, but I was too afraid of the answer.

She removed a glass bottle of milk from the fridge and

poured some into the smaller jug I'd placed in the middle of the tray. 'You do know I'd do anything for you, don't you, Martha?'

My lips parted with surprise. Feelings were not something we had ever discussed before. I wanted to return the sentiment, but the words stuck in my throat. 'I wish I had a lovely cake to offer the detective.'

'Not everyone can bake,' Ruby said. 'Just as not everyone can grow vegetables as well as you.'

'Maybe I should put a few carrots on a plate instead of cake.'

Ruby laughed loudly. 'Oh, Martha!'

'Shh,' I cautioned as I tried to stop myself from giggling. 'He'll hear us.'

Ruby took a deep breath. 'That's better.'

She looked at me and as soon as our eyes met, we burst into laughter once more. 'He'll either think we're quite mad or don't care one jot about what happened to Alice.'

'I think it's nerves,' Ruby suggested as she quietened. 'I feel very sorry for Mrs Warren, of course, but mostly I'm so very glad it wasn't you who dropped down dead.'

I wanted to say something in return, but I couldn't think of anything that would convey how grateful I was that we were both unharmed.

She walked around the table and grabbed one of my hands and squeezed it for a moment. Then we both looked away with matching looks of embarrassment. 'Do you think the kettle has nearly boiled?'

A few minutes later, we went into our small parlour. Stan and I didn't have many nice things, but I was very proud of the best room in our cottage.

'Here we are,' I said unnecessarily as I put the tray onto the low table in front of the striped green sofa where the detective sat.

Ruby perched directly opposite, leaving me the chair over by the window where I usually sat of an evening. 'Shall I pour?'

'Thank you, Mrs Miller.'

'Do you take milk?'

'Milk with two sugars, please.'

The politeness of our tones was stifling. I quickly poured his tea and handed him a saucer, then hurriedly made a drink for me and Ruby. I said a silent prayer that I wouldn't blurt out anything without thinking or say something that would cause the detective to think I was involved in Alice's death. The last thing I needed was to get myself into a bigger mess than the one I was already in.

'Let us start at the very beginning,' he said, his green eyes taking in my every feature. His close inspection left me feeling quite breathless. 'Tell me everything you did today.'

'We had breakfast,' I began. 'Ruby did my hair for me, and my make-up.'

'You went to the village green together?'

'Oh no,' I said. 'I went much earlier than Ruby. I needed to be there early. To help Mrs Warren... that is Alice... the deceased... set things up.'

I stammered to a close. Why hadn't I just said her name and left it at that? We all knew she was dead. I sounded cold, unfeeling, and much too matter-of-fact. Exactly how Ruby told me I'd acted when the detective arrived. Admitting to spending lots of time with Alice immediately prior to her death probably wasn't doing much to prove my innocence.

'I see.' He stirred his tea. 'Was there anything unusual about Mrs Warren this morning?'

'Nothing at all,' I blurted. 'She was her usual methodical self.'

'She didn't seem worried, or afraid of anything?'

'No,' I replied, wishing I could lie and put someone else in the frame. 'Everything was quite normal.'

'Talk me through what happened next. You got everything set up, then what?'

'We had different duties during the fete. I didn't see Mrs Warren until shortly before the prizes were to be announced.'

'Which was in the marquee?'

'That's right.'

'And what duties did you take care of during the afternoon?'

'It was my responsibility to make sure stallholders had everything they needed. Change to give customers, a pen to note prices, that sort of thing.'

'And Mrs Warren?'

'She took the judges around the marquee so they could look at the entries and decide which ones to award prizes to.'

He pulled out a notebook. 'Who were the judges?'

'Lord and Lady Chesden, they live up at the manor house. And the other judge is the MP, Rupert Gosford.'

'I will need to speak to them.' He jotted some notes, then placed his pen next to the saucer on the table. 'Where can I find the manor house?'

'Left out of here, past Farmer Bennington's fields, along the lane for a couple of miles. You can't miss it.'

'You didn't go back into the marquee?'

'I had no reason to.' That wasn't exactly what he asked. I paused as I tried to recall if I had gone in there for any reason. If I said I hadn't, and someone saw me, I would look guilty.

'Might you have gone in?'

'I don't remember,' I said quickly because I was convinced that not answering immediately made it seem like I was taking the time to make things up that were not true.

He stared at me, then bent his head to write in his notebook. I had done nothing wrong, yet I felt guilty. An uncomfortable flush began on my chest and quickly spread upwards to heat my face.

It wasn't only because I believed my gin was involved in Alice's death. It was also because of the way I was treated by Ada and Elsie. The height of my feelings of responsibility rose with every accusation levelled against me.

'I'm sorry,' he said, 'but I must ask you about the time that Mrs Warren died.'

He genuinely looked apologetic – as though he wished he didn't have to ask me the question. Usually we English bandy the word 'sorry' about in sentences without any real feeling. We apologise for everything – from someone bumping into us to expressing our regrets about the weather. Still, on this occasion, the detective seemed a little reluctant.

'Of course, Inspector.' I reached out to pick up my saucer from the side table, but my hands shook so badly I clamped them together on my lap. 'She took a drink from her glass, and soon thereafter slumped to the floor clasping her throat.'

'How soon after?'

'Well.' I thought for a moment. 'Immediately, really. Florence Noble, that's the publican's daughter, she passed around the drinks. I saw the horror on her face and then turned to Mrs Warren.'

'When you looked at Mrs Warren, was she already on the floor?'

'No, so it wasn't really instantaneous then, was it? But it all happened extremely quickly. I put my arms around her to try and help, but all I could do was lower her to the ground.' The words tumbled out of my mouth so rapidly it left me breathless. I shuddered as I recalled the events. For years, I lived through the uncertainty of the war, yet it wasn't until today that I had witnessed a person die. I knew and liked Alice, which made the whole experience so much more difficult.

'And you said she was grasping at her throat?'

'Yes,' I confirmed as I closed my eyes. Though, of course, that did not block out the awful images that played through my mind. 'As though she couldn't breathe. Her face turned the most awful colour.'

'Like a tin of Spam,' Ruby added. 'Sort of mottled. All pink and purple. It was frightfully upsetting for my sister.'

'And then?'

'The doctor arrived within a minute or so, but by that point, Mrs Warren was dead.'

'Can you think of anyone who would have wanted to hurt Mrs Warren?'

That hadn't even crossed my mind. I had been so fixated on my plum gin being the last thing Alice had drunk, I hadn't given a moment's thought as to why someone would want her dead. 'Alice and her husband were a quiet couple, but I believe they were universally liked around the village. I can't think of a single person who might want to hurt her, let alone kill her.'

'Where might I find Florence Noble?'

'She lives with her father in the village pub, the Cricketer's Arms. You can't think she had anything to do with this? She's only a girl.'

'She might have seen something useful I can use in my investigations.' He snapped his notebook closed, finished his tea and got to his feet. 'Thank you very much, ladies. I shall be back if I think of any more questions.'

* * *

Later that evening, Ruby and I ate a subdued supper and then sat together in the parlour with the wireless playing softly in the background.

'I'm sure you don't want to talk about it,' Ruby began, 'but we really must.'

I sighed. 'I don't know what more can be said on the subject.'

'Are you going to church tomorrow?'

'Of course,' I replied. 'Why wouldn't I?'

Ruby examined her nails. 'Do you think that's a good idea? I'm certain Mrs Harrington will have spoken to anyone that will listen, and that's before we consider Mrs Garrett.'

'I shan't let two bullies stop me from worshipping.' Determination not to be cowed made my voice harsher than normal.

'I think you should.'

'Ruby Andrews!' My sister refused to look up and meet my eyes. 'That would make me a coward.'

'It might also keep you safe.' Her bottom lip trembled so slightly I wondered if I had imagined it. Then she lifted her gaze to mine and there could be no mistaking Ruby's mood. 'I couldn't bear it if something happened to you, Martha.'

I shuffled my slippers on the carpet. Ruby was close to tears. I don't think I had seen her cry since one of our brothers held her favourite doll over the outside lavatory and threatened to drop it in.

'I'm sure I'll be fine, Ruby, please don't worry.'

'How can you say that?' Her face flushed as her voice rose an octave. 'Alice is dead. What if you're next?'

I wanted to tell Ruby not to be so melodramatic, but I couldn't think how to say it in a way that didn't sound cruel. 'If, as we suspect, someone used my gin to kill to Alice, then my life is quite safe.'

Ruby stared at me doubtfully. 'How do you work that out?'

'If I am being framed for murder, then it would be rather inconvenient for the real murderer if the chief suspect then died.'

She nodded slowly. 'I see. Yes, I do see that. You don't think it could've been an accident?'

'I can't imagine how someone could accidentally poison a bottle of my gin.' I shrugged. 'Surely people take care with lethal substances.'

A quiet knock sounded, and Lizzie lifted her head from where it rested next to my feet. Ruby and I looked towards the front door, then back at each other.

'I should answer that.'

'Yes, you should.' Ruby drew in a deep, shuddering breath and blinked away the tears pooling in her eyes.

I pushed myself to my feet and trudged to the door. Leaving the chain on, I opened the door a crack and peered through.

'Mrs Miller? Might I come in for a moment?'

I closed the door and released the chain with shaking fingers. I gave myself a moment to compose myself before I opened the door again. 'Of course, Vicar.'

Luke followed me into the parlour. Ruby got to her feet. 'I'll put the kettle on.'

'Is your sister all right?' he asked as Ruby slipped into the kitchen. 'She looks upset.'

'It's been a difficult day.' I put out a hand to indicate the sofa the detective had sat on earlier that day. 'Please have a seat.'

Although it was nice of the vicar to call around, it was a shame his visit had coincided with the personal chat between Ruby and me. Would I have got up from my chair and comforted my sister if he hadn't called round? Or would I have stayed in my chair berating myself for not moving whilst being quietly embarrassed at her show of emotion? I liked to think I would have chosen the former, but if that was the case, why was I sitting smiling awkwardly at the vicar instead of going to the kitchen to check on Ruby?

'Detective Inspector Robertson visited me before he left the village,' Luke said.

'Do you think he has any clues?'

The vicar looked uncomfortable. 'He didn't seem to have learned anything new.'

'Which means I am still the only suspect, if we are certain Alice's death was not an accident.'

'I'm afraid the detective thinks that is highly unlikely.'

I nodded because that was exactly what I'd said to Ruby. However, hearing that the detective thought the same thing made my legs feel weak. I felt as though I was trapped in the middle of one of those recurring nightmares, but the only difference for me was waking up would not bring any respite.

'Here we are!' Ruby's voice was overly loud as she strode into the small front room. 'Let's have tea.'

The quintessential remedy for all ailments – a good strong cup of sweet tea – was the last thing I felt like consuming. I had gallons of the stuff swishing around in my nervous stomach already.

'Lovely.' I smiled at my sister. 'Thank you, Ruby.'

'Shall I pour?' she asked brightly.

'That would be very kind.'

We sounded like we were taking part in one of those evening radio plays I sometimes listened to – all stiff politeness, lines delivered with very little feeling and no personal connection.

'I'm afraid I've come with bad news.' The vicar frowned as Ruby handed him his tea. 'I wanted to let you know straight away.'

'Of course,' I murmured. 'But how can any news be any worse than what's already happened today?'

'I shall just come right out and say it,' he said grimly. 'Mrs Harrington is insisting that the detective reopens the case into your husband's disappearance. She says that her husband knows influential people and will put pressure on the police until they comply.'

'How ridiculous,' Ruby said savagely. 'Why can't they just leave you alone? Who would do away with their husband and leave themselves destitute?'

I opened my mouth to argue with Ruby's choice of word, but closed it again. She was right. Stan's disappearance had left me penniless. 'Everyone in the village is aware of my financial situation. He should put a stop to his wife's malicious words.'

'I didn't know your circumstances were so difficult. Is there anything the church can do to offer assistance?'

'Thank you, Vicar, but no.' I smiled at Ruby. 'Now my sister is living with me, we manage quite nicely.'

Ruby looked pointedly at the drab housecoat and old slippers I had changed into after the detective left. Nothing about my appearance, or that of the house, suggested that we were well off.

'But is there anything that I can personally do to help?' he asked earnestly, as though he really cared – and not just because it was part of his job.

I had spent the afternoon ruminating on a little idea, and the latest news convinced me I should put my plan into action. 'Yes, Vicar, actually there is.'

'I would be glad to help.'

'You might not when you hear what I have to say.' I laughed nervously as I thought about his reaction. 'I need you to help me find out who killed Mrs Warren.'

Luke took a sip of his tea, his eyes not leaving mine. He swallowed and then nodded. 'I would be glad to.'

'You would?' I asked in disbelief, amazed that he agreed so readily. I had a personal reason to see Alice's killer uncovered, the new vicar did not.

'I know nothing about detecting, but I should be glad to help you clear your name. Do you think finding out Mrs Warren's murderer and clearing your name are one and the same thing?'

'I think they must be. Whoever killed Alice must surely have set me up to take the blame.'

The vicar leaned forward. 'Discovering other suspects may help to pinpoint the killer. Let that be the first item on our sleuthing agenda.'

'You believe in my sister's innocence?' Ruby raised a sceptical eyebrow.

'Almost everyone in the marquee drank your sister's home-made gin. Mrs Warren was the only person to die. She was obviously deliberately targeted. I can think of no motive your sister would have to kill Mrs Warren.'

'Other than becoming chairwoman of the village committee.'

'Is that position so prestigious it is worth murdering someone?'

'Not to me it isn't.' I shrugged. 'But perhaps it is to someone else.'

'But that wouldn't be their motive,' he said. 'Don't you see? Only you have that motive, and it's weak. We must uncover the real motive, and then we will have the murderer.'

'That sounds deceptively simple,' I said.

'I will try to see Charles Warren tomorrow. Ostensibly to offer my condolences, of course, but perhaps I can find out from him if he knows of any reason his wife may have become a victim.'

'It's definitely murder, I suppose?' Ruby asked in a tentative voice.

'From what I could see, it was a fast-acting poison. One wouldn't administer that by mistake, or to cause illness. Whoever it was meant for Mrs Warren to die.'

'I don't think I want you to investigate,' Ruby said in a shrill voice. 'You might put yourself in danger.'

'If I can't prove my innocence, people will always suspect me. Just as they have over Stan's disappearance. I must do everything I can.'

'You can count on me for support,' Luke said decisively. 'Don't worry, Miss Andrews, I will see that no harm comes to your sister.'

A warm feeling that had nothing whatsoever to do with the tea I'd consumed spread through my belly. This man... No, this *good-looking* man believed in me. Not only that, he assured my sister that he would take care of me.

The earlier doubt over my plan subsided, and I looked forward to working with the vicar to prove my innocence.

5

After church the next morning, I set out to the Cricketer's Arms to speak to the proprietor, Joe Noble, and his daughter, Florence. I was certain Detective Inspector Robertson would have spoken to them the day before, but I wanted to find out for myself if anything could have happened to my plum gin before Alice was poisoned.

Luke was to visit Ada Garrett and find out what she knew. As she was a terrible gossip, I expected she would be the best source of information in the entire village. Of course, she wasn't likely to tell me a thing given her unnatural hatred of me, so the vicar promised to use all his charm to extract any knowledge Ada may have.

I felt a little sorry for her to be on the receiving end of his substantial charisma. During an ordinary conversation, I was happy to answer anything he asked. If he were to make a concerted effort, as he intended to with Ada, I dreaded to think of what I would tell him. He had such pretty eyes, and his smile turned me into a bumbling idiot.

Marching down the lane in my usual sensible flat shoes and worn-out clothes, I wished I had a wardrobe full of dresses to choose from. They needn't be as pretty as the one Ruby had let me borrow the day before. Dressing up for the day had made me realise just how much I was missing out on by spending my days wearing men's clothing while I tended my garden. Vaguely, I recalled the days, pre-war, and before I met Stan, when I took for granted feminine clothes and shoes and my ordinary job as a typist.

In a dress, I had opportunities and choices. In my normal clothes, my life was filled with drudgery and monotony, with no hope of a reprieve.

Walking around to the lounge entrance of the pub, I pushed it open and went inside. Joe walked through from the bar and looked at me in surprise. 'Mrs Miller, what are you doing here?'

'I had to talk to you,' I said urgently. 'About my plum gin.'

'Keep your voice down! You'd better come through.' He motioned to the end of the bar, where he lifted a hatch. 'Watch the bar, Mavis!'

I followed him through to his private quarters, questions bouncing around in my brain. There were so many things I hoped he could tell me. 'Who is Mavis?'

'The barmaid. New girl from Edgecumbe. Very popular with the men of the village.' Joe winked. 'If you know what I mean.'

By that I understood Mavis was an attractive young thing who either wore her tops too tight or her skirts too short. 'Was she here at the pub when I dropped off my plum gin earlier in the week?'

'She only works weekends,' Joe replied. 'So no, she wasn't. By the time she arrived for work yesterday, Florence had already taken the bottles over to the village green.'

'Poor Florence, is she all right?'

'Had to give her a nip of brandy when she got back here. She couldn't stop shaking. The wife didn't know what to do with her.'

Joe was an enormous man, easily over six feet, with hands like shovels. By comparison, his wife, Winnie, was a petite little mouse of a woman. I didn't frequent the pub, but my nearest neighbour, Maud, had regaled me with stories about how Joe idolised his wife, and if she suggested he do something, he got up to do it before she'd barely closed her mouth. I wish I knew her secret. It would have been nice to have a husband who adored me instead of one who only seemed to notice me if I did something he didn't agree with.

'I wanted to ask you and Florence some questions, if she is feeling up to it?'

'Aye,' he said. 'I'll fetch her.'

He walked to the door of the small but neat living room and shouted for Florence. Taking his seat once more, he looked at me expectantly.

Trying to remain calm, I went through the things I wanted to know in my mind. How I wished I had the aid of a small note-book like the one used by Detective Inspector Robertson and Cyril Bottomley.

I cleared my throat. 'Joe, were the bottles of gin I brought here on Friday unattended until Florence took them out to the green yesterday?'

'No.'

I'd hoped for something more than a one-word answer. I licked my lips and tried again. 'So no one could have tampered with them?'

'Absolutely not.'

'How can you be so sure?'

'I put them straight in the cellar so they'd stay cool. I didn't want them in the corridor where anyone might stroll along and help themselves.'

'Do people usually walk along at the back of the pub, helping themselves to your alcohol?' I asked sceptically.

'Don't give them the chance,' he answered. 'I lock my cellar.'

Granted, I know nothing about the running of a public house, but locking a cellar seemed rather odd when a publican had to go down there frequently to change barrels and get new stock.

'Is that usual practice?'

'In my pub, it is.'

'Dad?' Florence stood in the doorway. When she saw me, her face dropped, then her expression turned mutinous. 'I don't know nothing!'

'Florence!' Joe pointed at the chair next to his. 'Sit.'

She walked into the room reluctantly, as though she was facing an executioner rather than one of her neighbours. 'Thank you for talking to me, Florence,' I said.

'I've already spoken to that detective. I don't know nothing, I've told you. Just like I told him.'

Although I didn't have children of my own, I'd spent enough time with my younger siblings to know when a teenager was telling an outright lie. They got angry, as if the person asking questions was the one in the wrong. Florence was also protesting way too much – another sign that she was certainly hiding something.

I looked at Joe and smiled in what I hoped was a reassuring way. 'Might I trouble you for a glass of water, please?'

'Of course, Mrs Miller.' He fixed Florence with a look as he stood. It was the age-old glare of a parent to their child, clearly transmitting the message: *don't you do or say anything to embarrass me in front of a guest.*

As soon as I was sure Joe was out of earshot, I leaned slightly forward in my chair and spoke in a low voice imparting gossip I had heard from Mrs Burnett. 'I understand you and Farmer Bennington's youngest son, Frank, have a special relationship.'

'What? No!' Florence flushed a deeper red than the lumpy sofa on which I sat.

For the first time, I was grateful I had occasionally listened to the gossip my neighbour, Maud, loved to spread. 'Quickly, before your father comes back. Might you have left the bottles somewhere yesterday while you went off to meet Frank John Bennington?'

'How did you know?'

'I didn't,' I said. 'Not really. Until I saw you just now, I hadn't remembered seeing young Frank hanging around the marquee. And, let's be honest, the Westleham Village Show isn't really a young person's thing, is it?'

'It's awful,' Florence agreed.

'Tell me everything,' I pleaded. 'It's terribly important. Everyone thinks I poisoned Mrs Warren.'

'Don't tell my father.' Florence cast a worried look towards the door. 'But you're right. Frank and I arranged to meet up. I left the bottles of gin and lemonade with the glasses just inside the marquee. Only for a couple of minutes, I promise.'

'While you and Frank had a little chat?'

'Yes,' she agreed readily. 'A little chat, that was it. For no more than five minutes.'

How long did it take teenagers to have a quick kiss and cuddle out of the sight of adults? I did not know. Stan and I had been to the pictures four times and dancing twice before he even dared to peck my cheek after walking me home.

'I think it might have been a little longer than five minutes.' Frowning, I did my best to look stern. 'I think you should tell me the complete truth, young lady.'

Florence looked frantically behind her. She looked close to tears. 'It might have been more like twenty minutes. And me and Frank might have had some of the gin.'

'You took a bottle for yourselves?' I asked in a gentler tone.

'Yes.' She looked down at her bitten fingernails. 'Oh, please, Mrs Miller. Don't tell my parents. They will be ever so angry.'

'I'm not cross about the bottle of gin,' I said carefully. 'But I am anxious about you being alone with Frank for such a long time. I would hate to keep your secret and then find out you had got yourself into *trouble*.'

'We didn't—' she stammered as she quickly realised my inference. 'That is. No, I'm not that type of girl. It was only a kiss. My mother would kill me if I was to bring shame on the family. And Frank is terrified of my father.'

With good reason. Frank was a stocky young lad and, as a farmer's son, was likely to be strong, but he was no match for a mountain of a man like Joe Noble. Yet Florence herself wasn't scared of what her father would say, but her mother. It seemed Maud's gossip was accurate – again.

'I'm very glad to hear it.' I sat back in my chair. 'Now, we'll make no more mention of it.'

Joe came back into the room and carefully placed a glass of water on a coaster on the table next to me. 'Is everything all right?'

'Yes, Father.'

'Have you asked all your questions, Mrs Miller?'

I took a sip of the water I asked for but didn't want. 'Just a few more, if it's not too much for Florence?'

Joe looked at his daughter, who nodded eagerly. 'Glad to help, Mrs Miller.'

'Is there anything at all you can tell me about yesterday that struck you as odd? Even if it doesn't seem very important. Anything at all?'

'Well, Mrs Warren had two glasses of gin. That's why I was so near the front when she... when she collapsed. She signalled to me she would like another drink.'

'Mrs Warren took a glass from your tray?'

'She did.' A sly grin crossed Florence's face. 'And she wasn't the only one who had a taste for your gin yesterday.'

'Now, Florence,' Joe said. 'Now isn't the time to chat about our neighbours.'

'I would appreciate you allowing Florence to answer,' I said to Joe as I took another drink of water to calm my nerves. Who knew interviewing people was so terrifying?

Joe nodded, and Florence smirked again. 'Mrs Harrington must have taken at least four glasses from my tray.'

'Mrs Harrington?'

'She does like a drink.' Joe nodded.

'Mrs Harrington?' I said again. 'Elsie Harrington, the postmaster's wife?'

'How many other Elsie Harringtons are there in the village?' Joe laughed.

'What do you mean by saying "she likes a drink"?'

Joe tapped the side of his nose. 'Let's just say, I know for certain she drinks more than a one-glass-after-dinner-amount of gin every week.'

That would explain her bizarre behaviour the previous afternoon. Though it hadn't even crossed my mind that Elsie had a drinking problem.

'One last thing.' I looked back at Florence. 'Did you drop the tray because you were so frightened at what happened to Mrs Warren?'

Florence frowned. 'Well, that's the strange thing, Mrs Miller. I can't swear to it, and perhaps I wouldn't have thought anything of it until you asked the question, but I rather thought someone jogged my elbow.'

'Causing you to drop the tray of drinks?'

'Well, yes.' Florence laughed nervously. 'But there was so much going on, I might be mistaken.'

I wasn't sure what relevance this could possibly have on Alice's death, but it was a peculiar event in a day full of very strange and troubling occurrences.

'Thank you very much.' I got to my feet. 'You've both been very useful.'

'Good day to you, Mrs Miller.'

One more thought occurred to me as I gathered myself to leave. 'How much of this did you tell the detective?'

Joe looked puzzled. 'We told him no one had access to the bottles, which is true. But he didn't ask about how much the ladies drank.'

'He didn't ask me about how I dropped the tray either,' Florence confirmed.

Whilst I was glad to have learned more information than the detective, it didn't help my quest to clear myself. So far as Detective Inspector Robertson was aware, no one had access to the bottles of gin except for me, the publican and perhaps his daughter.

I felt absurdly pleased that at least I was no longer the only suspect.

* * *

One thing I missed since Stan's disappearance was that I no longer cooked a Sunday roast after church. When we returned home from the service at All Saints' Church, Stan would sit in the parlour with the newspaper whilst Lizzie and I went through to the kitchen, where I cooked vegetables harvested from my small patch at the back of the garden and a small joint of meat. We could afford that little luxury on Stan's salary.

Ruby and I only had meat with our meals these days if it was a special occasion, or if I'd swapped some baked goods with Farmer Bennington. I had a ready supply of eggs from the chickens in the garden, but sugar was still rationed, so that seriously curtailed my ability to bake as much as I would like.

All that to say, it explained why, when the vicar called round to report on his visit with Ada Garrett, I was adding dumplings to beef stew that contained no beef.

'That smells delightful, if I may say so, Mrs Miller.' Luke came into the kitchen behind Ruby, who had answered the door.

'Thank you, Vicar. Would you like to stay for lunch?'

'Excuse me,' Ruby said. 'I'm going to walk into the village to make a telephone call.'

'Lunch will be ready in half an hour.'

'I'll be back.' Ruby gave a little wave from the kitchen door. 'See you later, Vicar.'

Luke rested on one knee on the cold stone floor to pat Lizzie.

'You'll end up as hairy as she is,' I said, nodding at the dog. 'Take a seat, Vicar.'

'I don't mind.' He regarded me thoughtfully, then looked back at my dog. 'However did you manage to feed her during the war?'

'I worked as a land girl,' I explained. 'Just up the road, on Farmer Bennington's land. He was grateful for the long hours I worked and let me have anything left from a slaughter that he couldn't sell. Lizzie learned to eat anything I boiled up with some vegetables.'

'You must be very resourceful.'

'I've learned to be.'

Talking about the things I had done to make ends meet embarrassed me. The vicar seemed to sense that and took a seat at the table. 'I will stay for lunch, if you're sure you have enough?'

'Of course.' I put the kettle on the range to boil. 'We might not have much, but we have an abundance of vegetables.'

'I'm afraid my housekeeper can't even boil water.'

I smiled. 'Yes, the previous vicar said the only reason he didn't starve to death was because of the number of meals he took at parishioners' houses.'

'This morning, she served burnt toast and hard-boiled eggs. Not even the birds would touch the toast, and the eggs were so well done, they bounced off the walls.'

'You didn't?' I giggled. Goodness, how long had it been since I had made that girlish sound? Too many months, I decided.

'I didn't,' he confirmed. 'But only because I was afraid she would catch me.'

'Isn't there anything you can do about her standard of work?'

'I don't believe there is. More is the pity. She came with the job, and the house.'

'What you need is a wife,' I blurted.

'You are not the first person who has suggested that matrimony is the answer to my woes. However, I understand that Mrs Johnson, maker of the delightful Victoria sponge, is already a married lady?'

Not for the first time, I wished I had a light hand with cake, but my talents didn't extend much further than simple things like boiling vegetables and making tea. However, I could make toast without burning it together with perfectly runny eggs as an accompaniment.

'Mrs Johnson is old enough to be your granny.'

He shrugged. 'Then it seems I am destined to remain single. At least while I live in Westleham.'

I couldn't resist asking him more. 'Haven't you seen any young ladies that have caught your eye?'

He followed my gaze towards the door Ruby left through. 'Like your sister, perhaps?'

Why was I always so transparent? This was why I had married a man like Stan. Flirting, being alluring, and all the other things men liked were not in my nature. Neither had I managed to master them. Ruby, however, was an expert at them all.

Ruby was also free to flirt with the vicar, and I was not. Luke Walker was about as out of bounds to me as the Duke of Windsor.

I lifted my chin. 'You could do much worse than Ruby, Vicar.'

'I'm certain your sister has loftier ambitions for herself than marrying a lowly village vicar.' He drummed his fingers on the kitchen table while he spoke, his eyes not leaving my face. I wasn't sure what he was looking for in my expression, but I did my utmost to keep it neutral.

Was I glad that Luke didn't appear to be attracted to Ruby? Yes, I was. The ache in my stomach eased as his words allowed the pang of jealousy to dissipate. More fool me. Ultimately, it made no difference if the vicar's affections lay with Ruby or someone else. It wasn't any of my business.

'I think you may be right.' I sighed. If she still lived with our parents, they would have persuaded her to marry the first eligible man in sight – as they had with me. Living with me gave Ruby a greater sense of freedom that I wasn't always sure was a good thing. If I tried to find out who she had telephoned this afternoon, she would change the subject. She did not confide in me.

The kettle whistled, and I walked over to the Aga. Pouring a little boiling water into the bowl resting in the sink, I added a sliver of soap. Over the years, I had learned that if you didn't clean dumpling mixture from a bowl very quickly, it set harder than concrete and took forever to remove.

'Tea?'

He pulled a face. 'I'm not sure I could manage another cup of tea. Mrs Garrett insisted I have two cups.'

'Mrs Garrett cannot make a decent cup of tea,' I said, then looked away quickly. My words were true, but maybe she had heard me say such a thing before, and that was the reason for her intense dislike of me? 'Why don't you try a cup of my lavender tea, Vicar.'

'I don't think I've ever had lavender tea before.' His face suggested he didn't want to sample it, either.

'I'll make you a cup. If you don't like it, I shan't be offended.'

'How did things go with Joe Noble at the pub?'

I placed the teapot on the table, together with cups and saucers. It would be a few minutes before the tea was ready to pour. 'Florence thinks someone jostled her elbow, and that is why the tray of drinks she was carrying fell to the floor.'

Luke leaned on the table. 'That's interesting.'

'It is,' I agreed. 'But Florence also confessed to me she met Farmer Bennington's son earlier in the afternoon, leaving the bottles of plum gin unattended.'

'So anyone could have tampered with them?'

'Yes, but it's more likely something was added to the glasses, isn't it?' I frowned, trying to make sense of the permutations. 'If the bottle was poisoned, more people would have died.'

'Unless the infected gin was in the glasses that were on Florence's tray.'

'But how could the killer have been sure only Mrs Warren would take a glass containing poison?'

'I don't think we *can* be sure of that.' Luke bounced his fingers along the table. 'Are we certain she was the target?'

'I can't think of any reason anyone would have to kill her. No one stands to gain anything.'

'Ah, well, that's not true.'

I lifted the lid of the teapot and gave the liquid a stir. Satisfied it was ready, I poured the tea into the two cups. 'What do you know?'

'Mrs Garrett said that she had heard from Mrs Harrington that Charles Warren stands to gain a sizeable sum of money from an insurance policy he had on the life of his wife.'

'How did Mrs Harrington know that?'

'Apparently from her husband.'

I mused over that information. 'Ernest Harrington is the postmaster, so it's possible that is the type of information he would be privy to. Joe Noble also told me that Mrs Harrington is a little too fond of the gin.'

'It's very possible she was a little loose-lipped and told Mrs Garrett something that she shouldn't have then, isn't it?' Luke pulled the saucer towards him and peered into the cup doubtfully.

I took a sip of my drink. 'See? There's nothing wrong with it.'

'I didn't think for a moment there was.' He took a cautious drink. 'I told you yesterday that I don't suspect you. It's the drink itself I'm not sure about, not you.'

I tried not to attach any meaning to his unerring belief in my innocence, but it gladdened by battered heart. 'Did you learn anything else from Mrs Garrett?'

He blew on the tea. 'Nothing that is useful.'

I heard the words that he was too polite to say out loud. 'I suppose that means she wasn't very complimentary about me?'

'She does seem to have a rather unhealthy hatred of you.'

I admired his honesty but couldn't help flinching a little at the word 'hatred'. It was so strongly negative. Not for the first time, I wondered what I had done to stir up such emotion from a woman I barely knew.

'I really don't know why.'

'I asked her. Do you want to know what she said?'

'What a ridiculous question,' I snapped. 'Do you know anyone who can resist finding out what someone else knows about them?'

'I'm sorry.' He blinked, pretty lashes closing momentarily over his blue eyes. 'That was very thoughtless of me.'

'So, do tell me. What is Mrs Garrett's reason?' I couldn't help the anger in my voice. It really was the most infuriating thing to be hated when you hadn't done a thing to deserve it.

'She said you didn't appreciate your husband, and it was your own fault he had gone off and left you.'

It was my turn to blink rapidly. I hadn't expected that. 'She doesn't dislike me because she thinks I buried Stan in my garden?'

'I think that's what she tells people, so she doesn't sound jealous.'

'Jealous?' I echoed. 'Of me?'

'You had a husband that came home from the war. She did not.'

My hand flew up to cover my mouth as I gasped. 'I didn't think. Oh, my goodness. Poor Ada.'

How could I have been so thoughtless? Perhaps because it was easier to write Ada Garrett off as a gossipy busybody than to examine why she involved herself in everyone's business. She was probably extremely lonely. I had been so wrapped up in my own life and troubles that I hadn't even considered Ada's.

'I prayed for her when I returned to the vicarage, and I also asked the Lord to comfort her.' Luke's mouth tilted upwards in a slight smile. 'But I also asked that she be forgiven for her transgressions against you.'

'Could she hate me so much she framed me?'

'I asked myself the same question,' Luke said grimly.

'And what conclusion did you come to?'

'I cannot rule out that scenario.'

I nodded. 'Yes, I see that. Perhaps we should set aside murder while we have lunch?'

'You're very kind. I hope it's better than this lavender tea!'

I looked at him indignantly. He winked so outrageously that we both burst into noisy laughter. Far from being insulted at his assessment of my tea, I saw his words for exactly what they were. He could see I was upset and had deliberately lightened the atmosphere.

If only that thoughtfulness didn't make me like him even more than I already did. I really must find something out about the vicar that would make him seem more human and much less of a complete dreamboat.

* * *

After lunch, Luke excused himself, saying he thought it was his Christian duty to visit Mrs Harrington after the state she had been in the previous day. Personally, I thought it was because he wanted to find more out about the juicy piece of gossip Ada had dropped in his lap. Could Charles Warren really have killed his wife for the insurance payout?

It didn't seem likely to me. They were a well-liked couple in the village, but mostly kept themselves to themselves. Other than Alice's role as chairwoman of the village committee, neither involved themselves in village life. Charles's extreme reaction to the loss of his wife seemed genuine to me. I couldn't imagine that someone who appeared to adore his wife as much as he did would have anything to do with her demise.

Ruby insisted I sit in the parlour while she took care of the dishes. Lizzie padded through to the other room with me and flopped in her customary place next to my feet.

'Fancy Ada being jealous of me because Stan came home from the war.' I shook my head and tutted. 'If only she knew.'

Reaching into the basket to the left of my chair, I pulled out my knitting. During the war, I'd knitted nothing but socks to send to Stan. He'd sent brief notes of thanks, of course, but I wanted more. I'm not sure I would've known what to do with passionate declarations of adoration – but I wanted at least some of the pretty language I'd seen in letters other soldiers had sent home to their sweethearts.

One girl I worked with in the land army received pages of beautifully written prose that I secretly thought her beau had copied from a book. Was it really possible such potent emotions could be felt by a chap sitting in a boggy trench somewhere in Europe? I wasn't so sure.

Looking at the pattern and the knitting hanging off the needles, I tried to figure out where I was in the matinee jacket I was working on. I didn't know anyone who was having a baby, but I'd bought the wool and the pattern not long after Stan had got home. For a few days, I allowed myself to believe one of the few times he'd squeezed into my single bed alongside me had resulted in a pregnancy. It hadn't, of course.

Nor was I likely to have a child of my own any time soon, given that it had been over nine months since he'd shared my bed, let alone disappeared on me. Yet another thing that made me so angry about Stan's desertion that I buried it as deeply as I could because it hurt too much to think about.

A few weeks ago, I found the long-forgotten yarn in a drawer and my mother's voice had come to me sharply: waste not, want not. And so, I was knitting the garment with no idea who I would give it to.

'Perhaps I should make it big enough to fit you, Lizzie,' I said.

My faithful companion thumped her tail on the floor enthusiastically. It did not fool me. Lizzie agreed wholeheartedly with everything I said, even when my ideas were ridiculous.

'Perhaps I should visit Margaret Leaming and see who won the prizes.' I consulted the pattern and started the next row. 'Maybe that has some bearing on who killed Alice.'

'How?' Ruby asked as she came into the room.

'I really don't know,' I answered honestly. 'Maybe someone didn't win a prize that they thought they ought to.'

'So they killed Alice so she couldn't award a prize to someone they believed wasn't worthy?'

'Possibly.'

'Is that an arm hole?' Ruby peered at my work.

'Not unless the child has arms as thin as a cocktail stick.' I held my knitting up to the light. 'It's part of the pattern.'

'Is it?' Ruby sat on the settee.

I ignored her. I knew little about knitting, but Ruby knew even less. 'Anyway, Luke thinks it's possible Alice wasn't the intended target. How could the killer be sure she would consume the poison?'

'Luke?' I looked over at her amused question. She waggled her eyebrows at me. 'Martha, do you fancy the vicar?'

I stabbed my needle into the next stitch and wound the wool around before glancing at Ruby. 'Of course not. What a silly thing to say.'

'You're blushing.'

'I'm flushed after cooking lunch,' I retorted, embarrassed to share with my sister how giddy I felt whenever Luke was around. She was forward-thinking enough to think it was perfectly acceptable for me to have feelings for another man, despite being married. I, however, was too ashamed to admit that I had never experienced the same excited, fluttery sensation in my stomach when I was around Stan.

'I'm not sure I follow,' she said. 'About the person who didn't win a prize killing Alice.'

'Thus far, we've been thinking logically by not seeing an obvious motive for Alice being murdered.' Talking and keeping my place in the pattern was impossible. I put the needles down in my lap and turned to Ruby. 'But maybe whoever killed Alice isn't rational.'

I didn't tell Ruby what Luke had learned about the insurance money Charles Warren was to receive. We didn't know if the information was correct. It didn't seem fair that I repeat what was essentially gossip. Especially when I knew how much it could hurt when you were on the receiving end.

'Good luck finding the village lunatic in Westleham!' Ruby chuckled. 'There are so many possibilities.'

I should tell Ruby that her language wasn't very kind. Certainly, there were several eccentric characters in the village, but calling them lunatics was probably a bit harsh. Then I remembered how much I hated it when our mother corrected me.

Ruby was an adult. It wasn't my place to tell her how to speak. After all, it hadn't done me any good following mother's advice, had it? I was stuck here, married to a man I hadn't seen in over a year. Meanwhile, Ruby ignored everything mother had ever told her to do and lived a wonderful life gallivanting off to London most weekends to meet some chap or other.

'I think I will visit Margaret.' I put the knitting back in the basket. 'She said yesterday she would visit me. I think I'll go to her.'

'Your knitting isn't going very well, is it?'

'What makes you say that?'

'Whatever it is you're making never seems to get any bigger.'

'It's a very complex pattern.'

'What would *Luke* say about you telling a lie?' she taunted with a grin. 'And on a Sunday, too!'

I picked up a pillow and threw it at Ruby.

Her laughter followed me as I closed the door and walked down the path towards the lane. If this was what it was like to have a proper sibling relationship, I decided I rather liked it.

6

Margaret Leaming's cottage was the first cottage on the main road into the village. Mine was the last on the way out, so we lived about as far away from each other as was possible to be in our small village.

As I approached the green on my left, I kept my eyes firmly on the path in front of me. I didn't want to look at the marquee where Alice had taken her last breath while lying in my arms.

On my right, I passed the pub, the post office and the haberdashery shop. The village was unusually quiet. I reminded myself it was a Sunday and most people would be inside sleeping off their Sunday lunch or enjoying the summer sun in their gardens.

Eventually, after walking past the bank on my left and other shops and houses, I arrived at the gate to Margaret's home. She was a relative newcomer to the village, and I knew little about her. Would she even be home, or would she be off visiting relatives? Not that a person could go far on a Sunday unless they owned a motor car, of course. Buses did not run to Westleham on bank holidays or Sundays.

I knocked on her door and looked at the parlour window to

the left. Lace curtains twitched, and I waited for Margaret to let me in. Long seconds passed before, eventually, I could hear her footsteps approaching. She opened the door little more than a crack and peeked out.

'Good afternoon, Mrs Leaming.' I smiled brightly to cover my shock. Margaret looked terrible. Her hair stuck out in all directions as though it hadn't seen a comb in weeks, and her face was pasty. 'I'm terribly sorry to disturb you with committee business on a Sunday, but there are a few matters I really must clear up.'

'Can't it wait?' she snapped, impatience tinging each word.

'I'm afraid it can't,' I said as pleasantly as I could. 'My liberty may well be at risk.'

'I suppose you had better come in then,' she said with no enthusiasm whatsoever.

I was puzzled. Yesterday, Margaret had been the only person who had been kind to me. Apart from the vicar, of course. What could have happened to make the committee secretary so reluctant to speak to me today?

She led me past the parlour and towards the kitchen at the back of the cottage. I wrinkled my nose as I followed her along the narrow hallway. The distinctive aroma of cat urine filled the air. Margaret stopped abruptly at the door to the kitchen and pulled the door closed.

'On second thoughts, let's go into the parlour.' She extended a hand. 'Lead the way, Mrs Miller.'

A tickle of fear feathered its way down my spine as I turned around. Was Margaret going to attack me now I had my back to her? No, Margaret and I had worked closely together for months now. If she were the homicidal type, I'm sure I would've had some sort of sign before now. I was allowing what happened to Alice to make me both paranoid and jittery as a result.

The parlour door was partially ajar, and I put out a hand and pushed it all the way open. The room was cluttered with furniture and, laid on every available surface, was a multitude of cats.

'Goodness,' I murmured. 'I didn't know you were an animal lover, Mrs Leaming.'

She entered the room behind me. 'Let me find you somewhere to sit.'

Torn between wanting to be polite and telling Margaret I would stand, I looked down at the carpet beneath my feet. Once I think it had boasted a flower-festooned pattern on a burgundy background. Now it was so covered in fur, it was extremely hard to tell conclusively. 'Oh please! Don't move them on my account. I don't mind standing.'

'Nonsense.' She scooped two cats onto the floor. Or it might have been three. Who was counting? 'Sit.'

I did as I was told. After all, I wanted information from Margaret and I determined that the best way to get what I wanted was to be as pleasant as possible. I wondered if she knew exactly how many cats she owned.

'What a lovely room.'

'I really should get rid of some of this stuff.' She picked a tea towel up from the back of the chair opposite mine and flicked it towards its feline occupants. With outraged meows, they stalked out of the room. 'But the furniture belonged to my late husband and I just can't bear to be parted with it.'

To my horror, tears filled Margaret's eyes. 'Are these his cats too?'

She blinked, and the moisture disappeared from her eyes. 'Goodness me, what a strange question.'

'I, I just thought,' I stammered, 'that as the other items in the room were his, that perhaps the animals were too.'

It was a remarkably stupid thing to say, but Margaret's unkempt appearance and her strange demeanour had me on

edge. Not to mention our friend and neighbour had been horrifi-
cally murdered the day before.

'I can't offer you tea. I'm afraid I have run out of milk.'

'Oh, that's fine, I shan't be staying long.' I didn't *want* to stay in
this stuffy house any longer than I had to. A glass of water would
have been welcomed after my walk, but if the kitchen was as
slovenly as the parlour, I'd wait until I got home. 'I thought of a
few questions last night and this morning and you're the only
person who can answer them for me.'

She sat heavily in the chair. 'Fire away.'

Margaret Leaming was one of those women of an indeter-
minable age. She could have been anything from late thirties to
early fifties. She usually fashioned her hair in neat, tight curls.
Ordinarily, she had a rather ruddy complexion and a figure that
would politely be referred to as stocky.

'Did you lose your husband in the war?'

She glared at me. 'I don't think you came here to talk about
my husband. I'm very busy, Mrs Miller.'

In other words: *ask me the questions you came here to ask, then
get out of my house.* Her attitude towards me was in direct contrast
with her sympathetic nature the day before. What had changed?

'I'm sorry, it's just that I hadn't realised until now you were a
widow. I—'

'Mrs Miller?' She looked pointedly at a carriage clock sitting
under layers of weeks-old dust on the mantelpiece.

'Sorry. I would like a list of everyone who was to win a prize at
the show.'

'How will that help you?'

I lifted a shoulder and smiled wryly. 'I don't know. Investigating is new to me. I'm trying to find out as much information as
I can, and hoping it leads to the murderer.'

'You're wasting your time.' Margaret's tone was kind, despite her words. She got to her feet and moved over to an attractive bureau in a corner of the room. 'There's nothing in the prize winners that will help you, but I have the list here.'

She handed me a sheet of paper, still attached to a clipboard. 'May I take this with me, or should I make a copy?'

'It isn't my decision.' Margaret eyed me shrewdly. 'You're the new chairwoman. It's up to you to decide whether those who were chosen as winners should still receive their prize.'

'Yes, thank you,' I mumbled, wondering if I would get to enjoy the position. I hadn't coveted the role, but if the rest of the committee agreed I should take over, I would carry it out to the best of my ability, despite the terrible way it became mine. But it would be hard being chairwoman of a village committee whilst sitting in prison – yet another reason to work hard at sleuthing.

'The other thing I wanted to know is if you noticed anything different about Mrs Warren? It's been suggested to me she consumed rather a lot of alcohol yesterday. Would you know if that was unusual?'

'I'm afraid I know Mrs Warren about as well as anyone else in the village.' Margaret hovered near my chair, clearly waiting to see me out. 'That is to say, not well at all.'

'Thank you, I'll let you get on with' – *cleaning your disgustingly filthy house* – 'your day.'

'Glad to have helped.'

'What a beautiful sideboard,' I said as I walked towards the door. 'It's incredibly eye-catching.'

The mahogany sideboard with its curved feet suggested it was Victorian. It had large compartments to each side with three drawers in the middle. In the centre of each drawer was a brass handle.

'Fake,' Margaret said quickly. 'I'm sure to people that don't know any better it looks like a real Sheraton, but it isn't.'

'I wouldn't know a Sheraton from a piece of furniture made by a high street carpenter. I'm not at all worldly, I'm afraid.'

She smiled and moved past me to open the front door. 'Well, good day to you, Mrs Miller.'

I inclined my head as I stepped onto the path leading down to the garden gate. 'Good day, Mrs Leaming.'

I drew in a deep breath as soon as she closed the door behind me. From her appearance and manner, I never would have imagined Margaret would live in such a slovenly way. She had a very capable air about her and looked like a cross between a fierce secretary and a strict governess. Nothing about her suggested she was an animal lover, let alone a cat collector.

I was quickly learning that I didn't know as much as I thought about the people who lived in Westleham. One of them was a killer – remembering that sobering fact made Margaret's feline obsession pale in comparison.

Someone had neatly trimmed the lawn on either side of the path. The hedge at the front of the property had also been tended to recently. I was as sure as I could be that Margaret must get someone in to do her gardening. There was no way someone who kept her home the way she did could otherwise have such a well-cared-for garden.

It may be a waste of time, but I added that to my list of things I wanted to find out. Who was Margaret Leaming's gardener and did they know anything about her missing husband?

* * *

The information I learned from one quick glance at the papers Mrs Leaming had given me led me to the house opposite mine. George Felton lived there with his wife, Gertrude, who worked as the housekeeper for the vicar. I had never heard George complain about his wife's cooking and I wondered if he was immune to it after years of marriage, or whether her poor skills only manifested themselves in the vicarage kitchen.

No one answered my knock on the front door, so I walked around the side to see if George was working on his garden in the back. As I unlatched the side gate, a bell jingled. I stepped back and dropped my hands to my sides.

George appeared moments later, a frown on his red face. 'Oh, it's you, Mrs Miller. How can I help you?'

'May I have a quick word?' I gestured towards the gate. 'I see you have rigged up some sort of alarm.'

'I didn't want the village saboteur to get my garden again.' He made no move to open the gate. 'I thought if I at least had a warning that someone was attempting to get in, I might have a chance of catching the blighter.'

'Ingenious,' I said. 'I wonder if Lizzie performs the same task for me. It does seem strange that our gardens have escaped relatively unscathed.'

'Unscathed!' George cried, his arms flapping animatedly. 'Did you not see the state the fiend left my broad beans in? No, you didn't, did you? Neither you nor Mrs Warren could be bothered to come and look at the destruction in my garden. You were both too busy putting on the village show for those who had produce left.'

With shame, now I remembered that George's garden was the first targeted by the vandal, but he hadn't made nearly as much of a fuss over the damage as he was doing now. Looking down at the clipboard, I found George's name and ran my finger along to the next column, which proclaimed the prize he'd won.

'There must be some mistake.'

'The only mistake that was made is allowing two females to be in charge of the village committee,' George raged. 'I said it at the time, and I shall say it again. We should reserve positions of such importance for men only.'

'How badly were your broad beans affected?' I kept my voice low and in direct contrast to George's irate tone, desperate not to give his lowly opinions of women in positions of authority any more credence.

'Are you deaf?' he asked stridently, as though testing my hearing. I wanted to back away further from the gate, but I wanted to hear his answer more. 'They were obliterated. The Nazis couldn't have done a better job of flattening them.'

'Really?' I raised an eyebrow and made no attempt to hide my sarcasm. 'Then can you explain how you were awarded first prize for them in the village show?'

His face changed from florid to dangerously dark red in seconds. 'Why, you conniving little witch!'

I wasn't sure how he could suggest I was the scheming one in our conversation. 'When the time is right, we will hold a meeting of the committee to see how best to proceed.'

'I demand my prize!'

'You have just told me a person unknown destroyed your broad beans.' I held the clipboard against my chest. 'Yet you were awarded the first prize for that very vegetable. I'm sure we can agree that the two facts are not compatible.'

'You made a mistake,' he said, pure venom making his eyes darker as he stared at me. He pointed a finger at me. 'You didn't hear me right. I said my runner beans were destroyed. Not my broad beans.'

'Mrs Leaming takes accurate notes of all committee meetings.' I stepped backwards. 'Those minutes were then typed up and distributed to all members, giving everyone a chance to report any inaccuracies. I am certain those notes will show the crop that you reported damaged was your broad beans.'

'You should think very carefully about what you do next,' he growled.

'Are you threatening me?' I asked with what was left of my bravado.

'No, I'm telling you, Mrs Miller.' He leaned over the gate and jabbed a finger wildly in my direction. 'It would be in your best interests to forget this conversation ever took place.'

Although this was the first village show since the war ended, I had heard all about the intense rivalries and open hostility shown between the villagers from Mrs Warren. I had believed her words of warning to be an over-exaggeration. However, it was apparent that she had underestimated the problem, because she was dead and, if I was any judge of character, George Felton would also like to strangle me here and now.

I hurried away from George, holding my breath until I was back in the lane. As I turned to latch the main garden gate, someone tapped my shoulder. I whirled around, brandishing my clipboard in the air as though intending to use it as a deadly weapon.

The vicar held up his hands. 'I'm on your side!'

His blue eyes were sad despite the note of joviality in his voice. 'I have just had the most disturbing experience.'

'Me too.' Luke swept an arm out in front of him. 'Shall we discuss it in the vicarage?'

I looked at his home doubtfully. 'Is Mrs Felton there?'

'I'm sure she will have left me a delicious cold supper and gone home to see to her husband.' He wrinkled his nose to show he expected his food to be anything but pleasant.

I couldn't decide which was worse – Mrs Felton being at the vicarage to overhear our conversation, or the vicar and I being alone in his home. Village gossip about me couldn't get any worse, but my naturally cautious nature took over.

'Perhaps I can fetch Lizzie, and we can take her for a walk together?'

He flushed slightly. 'Of course. That's an entirely more appropriate suggestion.'

I wasn't sure my reputation could get any worse, but it seemed ridiculous to take the chance of testing out that theory.

'I'll be back in a moment.'

I hurried across the street, wishing the walk with the vicar was merely sociable instead of one with the express purpose of pooling our information to uncover a killer.

* * *

'Let's walk up towards the farm,' I suggested after the vicar had given Lizzie a thorough petting. Perhaps I should have tested Stan around animals before deciding to marry him. I'd given Lizzie a home while he was away serving in the army. When he came home, he had never been unkind to her, but the way he studiously ignored her told me he disapproved of my decision.

'Less likely to send the curtains in the village into a frenzy of twitching if we go that way,' he agreed amiably.

'What have you learned?'

'I went to see Mrs Harrington. She was alone when I arrived and very talkative.'

'Oh dear,' I said. 'Was she vocal about her belief that I am a killer again?'

'She was keen to let me know that Mr Warren is to receive an enormous insurance payout following his wife's death.'

'Goodness, so that piece of village gossip was correct.'

'Is village gossip not usually accurate?'

'My husband isn't buried beneath my potatoes,' I said curtly.

'I think we've already established that,' he said easily, not taking offence at my abrupt tone. 'Otherwise, I might not be as keen to walk along a deserted path with you.'

I pointed into the ditch that ran alongside the narrow road on which we walked. 'If I was going to do away with someone, I'd shove them down there. They'd never be discovered. I think the only person who regularly walks this way is me – Farmer Bennington uses his tractor and Lord Chesden has a motor car.'

'What about Lord Chesden's staff? Don't they come down into the village?'

'That is a good point,' I said. 'Food is delivered to them, but I think you're right. Some of the staff do come down to the village on their afternoon off.'

'You wondered why I believed so easily in your innocence.' Luke put out a hand and rested it on my arm until I turned to look at him. 'You would make a terrible murderer. Your planning and ability to consider all eventualities is flawed. In my opinion, you're not nearly cunning enough.'

'What makes you the expert?' I asked with a grin.

Luke turned away from me and carried on walking. We had taken over twenty steps before he answered. 'I didn't realise until I served as an army chaplain just what men were capable of. It changes everything when you see the depths that some people will sink to. And I don't just mean the Germans, I mean Allied soldiers too.'

'Stan didn't talk about the war when he came home,' I said. 'I often wonder if something happened while he was away and that is why he eventually decided one day not to come home.'

'I don't think many men like to talk about their experiences.' Luke stared off across the fields of barley nodding in the slight breeze as he spoke. 'Do you think Stan is still alive?'

'Yes,' I replied immediately. 'Although I can't really tell you why I believe that so fervently. But I do. We didn't have an unhappy marriage, but I know I was not the love of Stan's life. I've always believed that he met someone else in London. Someone prettier, cleverer and altogether more entertaining.'

'Is it very difficult being tied to a man who has abandoned you so callously?'

'I can divorce him,' I said in a voice that sounded much stronger than I felt. 'In two more years, when it has been three years since his desertion.'

'Will you? Divorce him, I mean?'

'I don't know,' I said honestly. 'It isn't what a well-brought-up young lady does, is it? Though most of the village already thinks it's scandalous that I have *done something* to make my husband leave me.'

'Times are changing,' Luke said. 'Look at the Duke of Windsor.'

'I admire him so very much. He gave up everything for the woman he loves. I think that's what all young women hope for when they get married. That theirs is that type of powerful love.'

'I take it yours was not.'

'I'm embarrassed to admit that Stan and I rather fell into marriage. We were both single. The war started, and somehow I allowed myself to go along with the romance of it all. Not that there was anything at all romantic about war, or Stan and I. But, at first, that was how it seemed.'

'And when he came back?'

'We were strangers living in the same house,' I admitted sadly. 'Which is how Lizzie came to be my best friend. You know, I have never talked to anyone about these things before.'

Discussing my marriage with Luke didn't feel like a betrayal of Stan. I found it surprisingly easy to tell Luke things I'd never told another living soul. Other than Lizzie, of course, and she didn't really count. Saying the words out loud made them more real, and for the first time, I accepted how ill-matched Stan and I were. If only I hadn't been so keen to follow my parents' wishes and leave home and marry. Maybe if I hadn't been hasty, I would've found a man I could truly fall in love with. A man like Luke.

'You're not close to your sister?'

'I'm not,' I admitted. 'I'd like to be, but I don't think either of us knows how.'

'I disagree,' Luke said. 'I challenge you, Martha Miller, to go home this evening and tell your sister something you've never told her before. Anyone can see how that young lady cares for you. She's likely just waiting for a sign from you.'

'What should I tell her?' My breath caught in my throat as I allowed myself to hope that there was a way I could have the close relationship with Ruby that I wanted.

'Something personal that she doesn't know about you. Share part of yourself with her.'

'Goodness, is this the type of thing they teach you at vicar school?' I let out an embarrassed laugh. We were not from a family who shared their emotions or their hopes and dreams.

'No, it's what I learned being raised by a mother who prided herself on teaching her children how to love each other and themselves. It was a very important lesson.'

I couldn't imagine what it might have been like to have a mother like Luke's. Was it too late to learn the lessons she'd taught her son? I thought it might be quite nice to like myself a bit more than I did. 'Did your father learn that too?'

'My father was too selfish to find out anything about anyone other than himself,' Luke said harshly, before changing the subject. 'Now, about the Harringtons. As I said, Mrs Harrington was particularly talkative and only too happy to repeat the information about Charles Warren's insurance on his wife's life.

However, when Mr Harrington returned home, conversation dried up considerably. In fact, he was keen to reiterate his wife's recent ill health and he very quickly showed me the door.'

'Where had he been?' I accepted the abrupt segue of topic without comment. If the vicar wanted to talk to me about his father, then I was certain he would. Right now, he definitely did not.

'I don't know. I didn't ask him, and he didn't say.'

'Odd time for someone to go out,' I mused. 'Nowhere is open on a Sunday. Even the pub closes in an afternoon.'

'One thing is for certain,' Luke said. 'Mrs Harrington was exceedingly drunk, and Mr Harrington was horribly embarrassed because of it.'

'We must find a way to speak to Mr Warren,' I said. 'Now we are sure he has a motive for killing his wife, we must investigate him further.'

'I have already planned to call on him tomorrow to discuss the funeral arrangements. You should come with me.'

'I might say there are some papers I needed for the committee.' I cringed as I spoke. 'No, I can't say that. It's horribly insensitive.'

'Just come along then and offer no explanations. Perhaps between us, we will uncover something else to help us in our quest.'

We reached the lane that led to Bennington Farm, and I turned back towards the village. The vicar was probably carrying out some sort of parish duty by helping me to prove I was not guilty of killing Mrs Warren. I no longer cared what his motives were. I was simply enjoying that he was choosing to spend time with me. It was more than that, though. The knowledge that he believed in me spread warmth throughout my body, and I felt truly alive for the first time in years.

7

I met Luke outside the vicarage the following morning, and together we walked to Charles Warren's cottage. Clutching the clipboard Mrs Leaming had given me the previous afternoon, I hoped we would find out something useful from the new widower. So far, all we had discovered was a jumble of information – none of which seemed connected.

'This is by far the worst part of my job.' Luke paused at the gate to the Warren house and faced me, a grimace distorting his handsome face.

'How do you comfort someone who has been through such an ordeal?'

'A steadfast belief in God,' he answered. 'I believe that Mrs Warren is now in His hands. Although that is no consolation to those who are left behind, I do hope that it is a comfort.'

'Was it difficult to maintain such a strong faith during the war?'

If he wished I hadn't asked such a personal question, it didn't show on his face. 'Almost impossible.'

Luke had seen first-hand the things that Stan had witnessed.

While I appreciated the detectives who investigated my husband's disappearance suggesting to me that perhaps his experiences had affected Stan's mind, I didn't think that was the reason he had simply failed to return home. I had always thought that Stan had simply met someone else and could no longer bear to return home to me.

Perhaps that said more about my own insecurities than it did about Stan's intentions. He went to work and came home on the same schedule every day. Realistically, I wasn't sure when Stan had the time to meet someone and have such a torrid affair that he decided he'd rather be with this other woman than me. Though, I had to admit, if Stan met someone who made his heart beat that little bit faster – the way mine did when I was around Luke – then maybe he had simply taken a chance.

That was still the more likely scenario. I couldn't see Stan harming himself. Though what did I really know about his war experiences and what damage that may have done to his mind? The sad truth was I didn't really know my husband, and he didn't – hadn't – really known me.

Luke opened the gate and stood back to let me walk up the path. I then took a step to the side to allow him to lift the impressive brass door knocker.

The door opened to reveal a dishevelled Charles Warren. He was unshaven, and his hair was greasy and unkempt. Striped pyjama bottoms poked out beneath a thick dressing gown.

'Good morning, Mr Warren.' Luke looked at his watch. 'Am I early?'

'I expect you are quite on time, Vicar.' Charles looked at me and then at his attire. 'Do excuse me, Mrs Miller. I was not expecting you.'

'Please don't worry on my behalf,' I said. 'I can return home if you'd rather I didn't come in, but I very much wanted to pay my respects.'

He opened the door wider. 'Come in, both of you.'

Charles showed us through to a neat parlour that was stylishly decorated. Two armchairs sat on either side of the fireplace with a small sofa facing it. A huge painting of a countryside scene dominated the wall above the mantelpiece. Although I knew absolutely nothing about art, I knew I liked it very much.

'What a beautiful picture.'

Charles looked up, as though shocked to see the painting hanging on the wall, and then his face crumpled. 'Alice fell in love with it on our honeymoon to Scarborough. It was a frightfully large amount of money, but I couldn't tell her she couldn't have it. I never learned how to say no to her. And now she's gone. Oh, what am I to do?'

I clamped my mouth shut. Why was it I always said the wrong thing? Whether it was questioning the vicar about things that were none of my business, or goading George Felton into threatening me, it seemed I was always talking myself into trouble.

'Mr Warren,' Luke said soothingly. 'Is there anything we can do for you?'

Charles looked aghast. 'I haven't offered you tea, let alone a seat. Please sit down, and I shall put the kettle on.'

'We don't need tea, Charles,' Luke told him. 'We have come to see if there is anything *you* need. And I wondered if you might be ready to talk about a service for your wife.'

Charles pulled a handkerchief from his dressing-gown pocket and mopped his eyes before blowing into it. 'I can't bury Alice until after the inquest.'

I didn't know they had arranged an inquest. Though I suppose it was to be expected in a death that was both sudden and unnatural.

'Do you have any family who can accompany you to the inquest?' Luke asked. 'I should hate to think of you going through such an ordeal without support.'

'There's no one.' Charles shook his head. 'Just me and Alice.'

'If you would like, I shall come to the inquest with you.'

'That would be very kind, Vicar, thank you.' Charles looked at me. 'What about you, Mrs Miller? Will you be there?'

'I rather think Mrs Miller will be required as a witness.'

Goodness. Why hadn't I thought of that? 'Will I?'

'Almost certainly,' Luke said. 'You were in close proximity to Mrs Warren when the incident happened, and I am sure the coroner will need you to tell him exactly what happened.'

'You will do that, won't you, Mrs Miller?' Charles turned to me, his eyes beseeching. 'For my poor Alice.'

'Of course,' I agreed. I didn't think any witness at an inquest had much choice about their attendance. Not that it mattered. I would be glad to tell exactly what I knew and could only hope that it was of some use. Certainly, the knowledge I had so far wasn't doing me a lot of good. Perhaps the police would have more luck in piecing together exactly what had happened.

'You should take all of Alice's committee papers home with you.' Charles jumped to his feet. 'Alice would want you to have everything. Especially as you will take over.'

His words ended on a sob as he hurried from the room. I looked at Luke. 'An inquest?'

'That's a good thing,' he whispered. 'Hopefully it will stop the nasty gossip about you.'

'If the police come to the same conclusion you have that I had nothing to do with it.'

'Don't be so negative,' he told me. 'You did nothing wrong. Hopefully the police will see that Alice's killer could be almost anyone in the village.'

'Here we are,' Charles said in a falsely bright voice. He put one of the crates the village shop used for storing vegetables at my feet. 'This is all the paperwork for the committee. Alice kept everything.'

'Thank you, that's very kind, but—' I broke off as Luke nudged me with his elbow. I looked at him and he gave a slight shake of his head. Was it possible he could read my mind and know that I was about to say I didn't know if I was going to be the next chairwoman of the village committee? That it rather depended on whether they charged me with the murder of his wife?

'I'll carry it over to your house for you, Mrs Miller,' he said. 'It looks very heavy.'

'I expect everyone thinks I did it,' Charles blurted out.

'What on earth do you mean?'

'I saw Mrs Garrett last night when I went to use the telephone.' Charles rubbed a hand over his eyes. 'I needed to let work know I wouldn't be in today. Anyway, she told me that there are rumours all over the village saying I killed Alice for her life insurance.'

'Oh, but Mr Warren, that's just plain ridiculous!' I said instinctively, moved by what I believed was his genuine distress. Killing Alice for her life insurance was a very good motive, but could Charles really have done something so mercenary?

'Mrs Miller is right. You shouldn't listen to idle chatter. It can be very cruel.'

'You shouldn't let what other people think of you upset you.'

'Shouldn't I, Mrs Miller? Aren't you distressed when you hear that people have suggested you did away with Stan. *I loved my wife.*' The insinuation was there, though not spelled out, that he loved his spouse whilst I did not. I couldn't correct him because he wasn't wrong. I was fond of Stan, but I had long ago accepted that I didn't have the sort of love for him that a normal wife should.

'I'm very sorry.' I looked down at my lap.

'You don't have to apologise.' Charles sighed. 'It's just that I find it very difficult to accept that people who I have called friends for years have not come to the house to offer their commiserations. I know why now, don't I? It's because they all think I am going to be a rich man because I've done a terribly wicked deed.'

'Have you spoken to the police about the insurance policy?'

I held my breath, waiting for Charles's answer. Luke was so clever. He'd queried the veracity of the gossip without coming right out and asking about it.

'I told Detective Inspector Robertson about its existence immediately.' Charles put his head in his hands. 'However will I hold my head up around the village?'

'The easiest way to do it is one day at a time,' I said earnestly. 'Just carry on your normal life, and eventually the gossip will move on to someone else.'

'That's good advice,' Charles said in a broken voice. 'I will do that tomorrow. After all, I am expected back to work.'

'Surely they will let you have longer off in the circumstances?'

'I'm sure my employer would have, Vicar,' Charles replied. 'But I told them I would be back tomorrow. Mrs Miller is right – I need to get back to normal as quickly as possible.'

He tried to smile, but it was more like a grotesque baring of his teeth. He held the expression for a moment before breaking down once more and sobbing into his hankie.

* * *

I walked back to my house with Luke after Mr Warren had assured us there was nothing more we could do for him.

Luke placed the box containing Alice Warren's papers on the table in my kitchen. 'I should probably get on with parish duties. Maybe get a start on this Sunday's sermon.'

'I think yesterday's was well received.'

'Was it?' Luke braced his hands on the kitchen table. 'I can never be sure.'

'I always think you can count a sermon as a success if the majority of the congregation are awake when you've finished speaking.' Putting the kettle on to boil, I returned to the table and leafed through Alice's committee documents. 'I'm not sure I understand Alice's filing system.'

Luke peered into the crate. 'There doesn't appear to be one.'

'I need to find the notes from the meeting held in April.'

'I don't mind helping you look. Surely it counts as helping a parishioner?'

Smiling, I passed a handful of papers over to him. 'If you're sure you don't mind, I would appreciate the help.'

'What, exactly, am I looking for?'

'Handwritten notes. Mrs Leaming types up the minutes from her notes. I checked my copy yesterday after I spoke to George Felton. They only mention that he complained about some of his crops being damaged. I'm hoping Mrs Leaming noted the particular vegetable he claimed was destroyed.'

'Claimed?'

'I believe George is the person who has been vandalising gardens in the village.'

'George, husband of my housekeeper?' Luke frowned. 'Why do you think that?'

'I visited Mrs Leaming yesterday after church. Which, let me tell you, was an experience all of its own. Have you visited her cottage yet?'

'No. I have a list of everyone in the village and am slowly getting around to seeing everyone. Is there something I should know?'

'Mrs Leaming likes cats.'

'I like cats,' Luke replied.

'I can guarantee you don't like them as much as Mrs Leaming.' I lowered my voice, even though we were the only two people in the house. 'She has so many I couldn't count them all.'

He motioned for me to continue with his hand. 'And? I am sensing there is more to this story.'

'Please don't think me a terrible gossip, Vicar,' I said, because of his opinion of me mattered very much. 'But the animals were very unsanitary. In addition, Mrs Leaming herself was not as presentable as normal.'

'Was she not at church yesterday?'

'If she had attended in such a dishevelled state, she would have been the talk of the village before the first reading.'

'Does she usually attend regularly?'

I thought for a minute. 'No, she doesn't. Still, after the village show, it was strange that she wasn't in attendance.'

'Why is that?'

'They shut the shops on a Sunday, Vicar,' I explained. 'I'm sad to say that most villagers get their daily dose of village comings and goings at church. After Alice's death, even more so than usual, I expected the church to be full.'

Luke lifted a shoulder. 'I don't mind how I get them through the doors, Mrs Miller. I'm just glad the attendance was so good. It *was* good, wasn't it?'

'It was a decent turnout,' I confirmed. 'Though I expected that because, first, it was your first service, and second, people would want to hear the latest about poor Mrs Warren.'

'Here!' He held a single sheet aloft. 'Mrs Leaming's writing is quite terrible, but she notes that "Mr George Felton made an official complaint about his entire crop of broad beans being destroyed by a person or persons unknown".'

'I knew it,' I said triumphantly.

'Why is that important?'

'Because Mr Felton won first prize for his broad beans in the village show.'

'Ah. I see why that is a problem. What will you do?'

'I think I must telephone Detective Inspector Robertson and let him know what I have found.'

'Is it possible Mr Felton killed Mrs Warren to keep his prize?' Luke asked, a doubtful expression on his face.

'Everything is possible, Vicar.' I crossed to the hob where the kettle was merrily whistling. 'Tea?'

'Only if it isn't herbal.' He wrinkled his nose. 'Why do you drink that stuff?'

'If I don't use the coupons for tea and sugar in my ration book, I can get extra meat for Lizzie.'

'In that case, I shall take one of your cups of herbal tea.' He grinned.

'I appreciate your sacrifice, Vicar, but I can use Ruby's tea. She will never know.'

'Ah.' He raised a finger into the air. 'But I shall know. Herbal tea for me. Perhaps I will grow to love it. Now, about Mr Felton?'

'Oh, I think silencing Mrs Warren is a very likely motive. His demeanour was quite alarming. I wouldn't put killing her to keep his prize past him.'

'Perhaps you should not be going about the village interviewing people by yourself.'

'It is very kind of you to worry about my safety.' I placed the lavender pods into the tea ball and poured the boiling water over the top. 'But I am used to looking after myself.'

'I'm sure that is true,' he replied. 'Though not while there is a murderer on the loose in the village.'

'We can't do it together,' I said. 'I am certain someone will have seen us walking Lizzie yesterday. Then today we are together again. Haven't you ever worked in a village before?'

'Of course. Though in my previous parishes, the female members of the community were mostly as old as my grandmother.'

'Then you must take more care of your reputation,' I said earnestly. 'Mine is destroyed, so I know how easily it can happen. You have carried a box over for me this morning. A neighbourly cup of tea is acceptable, but you must leave in the next fifteen minutes, otherwise I can guarantee there will be chatter about your morals before the butcher closes for lunch.'

'Is it really that bad?'

'I'm afraid so.' I brought the teapot over to the table and fetched two cups and saucers. 'So we must talk quickly. What is our next move?'

It felt quite delicious to use the word 'our' and I held my breath, waiting for his answer.

'You are to telephone the detective. Perhaps I—'

A knock on the door interrupted Luke's words, and I raised my eyebrows at him. 'See? I told you.'

I hurried to answer the door to find my neighbour on the other side. 'Good morning, Mrs Miller. I wonder if I might have a moment of your time?'

'Come on through to the kitchen, Mrs Burnett. The vicar has kindly just carried over a box of committee papers of Mrs Warren's for me to go through. Would you like a cup of tea?'

'Oh, that would be nice.' Maud Burnett, my next-door neighbour, fanned the air in front of her face. 'It's an extremely warm day again.'

'Yes. I've neglected my garden the last few days. I expect the sun has caused the weeds to grow even more quickly than normal.'

Maud walked into the kitchen in front of me. 'Oh, fancy seeing you here, Vicar!' she exclaimed in a surprised voice, as though I hadn't told her he was here only moments earlier.

'Mrs Burnett, isn't it?' Luke got to his feet and pulled out a chair for my inquisitive neighbour.

'How is Mr Warren bearing up?' Her words proved me right – she knew exactly where we'd been.

'About as well as can be expected,' Luke said. 'He told us they expect him back to work tomorrow.'

'That's too soon,' Maud tutted as though her opinion was the only one that mattered. 'Much too soon. Perhaps what I've been hearing about that man is true.'

'What have you heard?' I asked before I could help myself. 'Is it information that we need to pass on to the detective? Might it help the investigation?'

'I believe he's already aware,' Maud replied, looking between Luke and me and drawing the moment out for as long as possible. 'He also knows about the insurance due to Mr Warren.'

'There's something else?' I no longer made any effort to pretend I was only interested in the information so far as it pertained to the case.

'There is!' Maud announced triumphantly. 'I heard that Mr Warren has a lady friend in the city.'

'Surely not.' I shook my head. 'Mr Warren seemed genuinely distressed. I can't believe that of him.'

'Mrs Miller,' Maud said, voice laden with pity, 'if anyone

should understand a gentleman's practice of having a *special friend* as well as his spouse, it should be you.'

I flushed and looked down at the table. 'I'm sure Stan didn't—'

'That's because you're his wife, dear.' Maud patted my hand. 'It was very clear to everyone else that your husband's affections were, very sadly, elsewhere.'

I wanted to carry on with my denial and insist that Stan wasn't that sort of man and that my husband wasn't capable of such duplicity, but I couldn't. Not when I knew her words were more than likely the truth. I was glad that at least one person in the village could see that my marriage was over – and not because I'd lost my temper with Stan and buried him underneath my potatoes.

'Mrs Garrett believes the loss of my husband's regard was my own fault.'

Luke squirmed in his chair, and I regretted my thoughtless words. He had told me what Mrs Garrett said. I wasn't making things any better for anyone by repeating her words. Least of all him.

'Rubbish!' Maud declared. 'You did your best. Now you should do what Mrs Simpson did and get yourself one of those divorces. I shouldn't think you'll do as well as her and get yourself a prince next, but perhaps you can find a much nicer fellow who will give you a whole house full of babies.'

I didn't think I could get any more embarrassed, but I was wrong. Mortification barely covered it. The last things I wanted to discuss in front of Luke were my husband, our marriage and my inability to produce children despite our lengthy union. Notwithstanding, of course, that Stan had been abroad for much of our married life.

'Thank you, Mrs Burnett,' I mumbled. 'I will certainly give your advice some thought.'

'Perhaps I could help?' Luke offered.

'You?' I squeaked.

'Some people dislike talking to the police,' he said. 'Perhaps if I visit your husband's employer, they might talk to me. People rarely mind chatting to a vicar.'

'Oh no, I couldn't let you do that.' I shook my head for emphasis. 'Though it's very kind of you to offer.'

'Nonsense, it's an excellent idea!' Mrs Burnett clapped her hands together. 'You must go to London tomorrow, Vicar. How will Mrs Miller ever find herself a more suitable husband while she remains married to Stan?'

'I'm sure the vicar has better things to do, Mrs Burnett,' I protested.

'Hogwash.' She clasped a hand to her heart. 'All you have to do, Vicar, is find some evidence that would allow Mrs Miller to be released from her dreadful marriage, then she can be happy again.'

'I really don't think—'

Maud waved a hand in front of my face. 'You think too much. Wouldn't you be happier knowing what happened to Stan?'

'I would be glad to help,' Luke said. 'If you agree, of course, Mrs Miller?'

Actually, I thought it was a perfectly awful idea. One that would only make things worse. I preferred to busy myself in Westleham and try to put Stan out of my mind. Although I believed Mrs Burnett was right, and my husband had run away to be with another woman, I had no desire to be proven correct. No woman wanted categoric proof that they could not keep their husband from straying.

I looked at Luke, who smiled and nodded encouragingly, to

Mrs Burnett, who simply looked hopeful. What would it be like to be free of Stan and our dreadful marriage? Would that give me the courage to see if my fledgling friendship with Luke could become something more?

I also wanted to follow Charles Warren and see if there was any truth in the gossip about him. Perhaps I could happen to be on the same train as Luke. 'If you are sure you don't mind becoming involved, I would be grateful, Vicar. Maybe it's better that I know the truth instead of living in limbo. Shall you get the commuter train into London?'

Luke got to his feet. 'Yes, I will. Now, if you ladies will excuse me, I should get on. There is so much to do when one is new in a parish.'

'Such dedication.' Maud put one elbow on the table and positively swooned.

'I'll see you out.' I turned to Luke before I opened the door and whispered, 'I shall be on the same train in the morning.'

'I rather thought you might, Mrs Miller.'

* * *

Early the following morning, Ruby and I left the house together to walk the short distance to the train station. Once we reached Slough, Ruby would go to work as normal and I would remain on the train to its destination of Paddington.

The previous evening I had used the telephone box next to the post office to leave a message for Detective Inspector Robertson outlining what I had found out about George Felton and that I believed him to be the person responsible for vandalising gardens in the village. I hoped that he would deal with that situation while I was away for the day.

'There's Mr Warren,' Ruby commented, looking out of the

window as we settled into our seats. 'He looks dreadful. I really don't think he's having an affair.'

'Do you think it's possible to tell?'

'Almost always,' she said decisively.

'Do you think Stan was involved with someone else?' My heart hammered in the same rhythm as the train as it sped along the tracks and I waited nervously for her answer.

'Why are you asking about him now, Martha?' Ruby looked at me with concern.

'You know so much more than me,' I said. 'About people and relationships and the like.'

'I didn't really see you and Stan together often enough to form an opinion of him,' Ruby said carefully.

'But what you did know of him?' I pressed.

'Why is this so important to you?'

'If he was having an affair, I could divorce him.'

'You could,' she said slowly. 'But would you? What has made you think about divorce?'

'Maud Burnett,' I confessed.

'Maud, or the very dishy new vicar?'

'Both,' I admitted before I could change my mind and make something up.

'Well, I'm pleased.' Ruby smiled at me. 'You've spent enough time being sad, Martha. It's time to live your life.'

'It's only been a year,' I protested.

'He's only been *missing* a year,' Ruby corrected. 'But you've been unhappy for much longer than that.'

I wanted to deny her words. Usually, I would have allowed loyalty to my husband to tell Ruby she was wrong. But remembering Luke's advice about my relationship with Ruby, I decided to tell the truth. 'You're right. It's very hard to admit it, but we did not have a happy marriage. Maybe it is time for me to leave Stan and our marriage behind.'

Ruby looked at me in surprise. 'Was that very difficult to confess?'

'Yes,' I said. 'It's not the done thing, is it? Us Brits just say everything is all right, even if it isn't.'

'I'm sorry you and Stan weren't happy, Martha.'

'Is that why you haven't married yet? Are you worried about making a disastrous match too?'

'If I had stayed at home much longer, I'm sure Mother and Father would have insisted I find a man to look after me. I was very grateful to receive your letter and escape.'

'They're not bad people.'

'No, they're not,' Ruby agreed. 'They just needed more space for our younger siblings. But I won't let that rush my quest to find a chap to sweep me off my feet.'

'None of the ones you go to the pictures with have done that yet?'

'No.' She looked out of the window. 'Not yet.'

There was something she wasn't telling me, and I wanted to know what it was. I thought desperately of some way of asking her, but I couldn't find the words. After too many years of being taught not to discuss emotions, it was hard to break that cycle.

The train pulled into Slough, and Ruby leaned forward and kissed my cheek. 'See you tonight, Martha.'

Warmth spread through me at my sister's unexpected action. I blinked away stunned tears just in time to see a man catch hold of Ruby's arm as she walked along the platform. There was something proprietary in the way he held on to her. As the train pulled out of the station, I caught sight of Ruby's face. She was turned away from the man, but I could see her expression clearly. To my dismay, her pretty face was a mask of misery.

8

Luke waited for me to disembark the train on the busy Paddington platform. He caught my arm. 'Quickly, Mr Warren has already left the train.'

With our arms linked, we hurried through the throngs of people. Most were men with briefcases, smart hats and shiny shoes, heading for the offices of London. There were a few ladies who looked dressed for a day's work, and several who appeared to be there for shopping. However, they all had one thing in common and that was that they walked by so caught up in their own lives and schedules that they paid me and the handsome vicar at my side no mind.

'Can you see him?' I asked as we reached the bottom of a flight of stairs.

'Yes, let's hurry.'

Luke motioned for me to go up the steps before him. At the top, I was rather out of breath. He caught hold of my arm once more as we emerged into the daylight.

A few minutes later, Charles Warren entered a building. Luke and I came to an abrupt halt outside. 'What now?'

'I shall go inside and enquire after him.'

'Won't that be rather obvious?'

'I will say we are friends. I caught sight of him on the street, and I should like to meet him for lunch. It's not completely untruthful.' Luke looked at me with a worried expression. 'Will you be all right here by yourself while I go inside?'

'I frequently come to London by myself.'

He looked at me doubtfully. 'If you're sure.'

I nodded, and Luke went inside.

He was right to be distrustful of me. 'Frequently' was rather a stretch. I had once come into the city to meet Stan after work for dinner with the manager of his department and some other colleagues. Emboldened by that one excursion, I had caught the train again a few weeks later and surprised Stan at his office. He had certainly been shocked, but he was not pleased.

'How did it go?' I asked when Luke came back outside moments later.

'Charles is a solicitor. He works for Marshall and Reynolds up on the third floor.'

'What do we do now?'

Luke looked over my shoulder. 'There's a café across the road. Shall we sit in there and see what he does at lunchtime?'

'It could be hours until he comes out for lunch.'

'We didn't really plan this very well, did we?'

I laughed. 'Not at all.'

'Mrs Miller.' He indicated the café opposite. 'Let me treat you to a cup of tea. A cup of *real* tea, with as much sugar as you like.'

It sounded heavenly and took me no time at all to give my answer. 'I would be delighted. Thank you, Vicar.'

We found a pedestrian crossing and hurried across the road. He held the café door for me. When we were seated, he turned to me with an earnest expression. 'Do you think, while we are away from the village, that we might call each other by our Christian names? It sounds so stuffy to call you "Mrs Miller", even though I know we have only known each other a matter of days.'

'I don't suppose it would hurt,' I agreed.

A waitress came over and smiled brightly at us. 'What can I get you?'

'What will you have, Martha?'

Luke's eyes sparkled as he said my name. For a moment, I forgot I could talk. Pushing aside my worries that our fledgling relationship wasn't entirely proper, I cleared my throat. 'I'd like a cup of tea and a cheese scone, please.'

'I'll have the same, thank you.'

The waitress bobbed her knee. 'Right you are, sir, madam.'

Was it wrong to pretend, just while we were in the café, that I wasn't Mrs Martha Miller of Tulip Cottage, Westleham and Luke wasn't the Reverend Luke Walker of the same parish? Could I maybe imagine I was simply a normal young lady, and he was a splendid chap that wanted to get to know me better?

The door opened behind Luke, and a man I vaguely recognised entered the café. 'Mrs Miller? Martha Miller, is that you?'

Luke looked at me warily. 'Who is it?'

I didn't have time to answer his whispered question before the man made his way over to our table. 'Hello.'

'It *is* you.' He beamed at me as though we were long-lost friends while I struggled to place his face and conjure up his name from the depths of my memory. 'It's been... Goodness... How long?'

'Quite some time,' I murmured.

'I suppose it was that dinner.' He gave an awkward cough. 'Those work events are always so tiresome, but one can't refuse to attend.'

I still couldn't recall his name, but he had told me enough for me to remember that he was one of Stan's colleagues.

'I thought the food was quite delicious,' I said honestly while frantically grasping for something else to say that didn't make me sound like a complete idiot.

'Do you mind awfully if I join you?' He directed the question at Luke.

'Of course not.' Luke indicated a spare chair. 'Please do. I am Mrs Miller's vicar, Luke Walker.'

'Pleased to meet you, Vicar.' The man in his smart suit shook Luke's hand. 'Gilbert Newberry. I worked with Mrs Miller's husband at the bank before—'

He looked at me, distress clear in his eyes. 'Before Stan went missing. It's all right, Mr Newberry. The vicar knows all about Stan's sudden disappearance. In fact, that's the reason we're here in the city today.'

'Is it?' Gilbert Newberry looked at me with a frown. 'To what end?'

'I was rather hoping to speak to people that Stan worked with,' Luke said. 'My understanding of the situation is that the police could not uncover any reason for him to abscond so suddenly. I thought that perhaps if I were to speak to his friends they might be more open with me.'

'With you being a vicar?'

'Yes, indeed.'

'Do *you* know anything, Mr Newberry?' I asked, because suddenly, after so long of not knowing, and not wanting to know, I found that I desperately wanted a resolution. Ruby was right. I had been unhappy for long enough. It was way past time for me to take some control of my miserable life.

The waitress returned with our order and took Mr Newberry's. He waited for her to leave again before he spoke. 'Only what I told the police.'

'Which was?'

Gilbert shifted uncomfortably in his seat, and he pulled a finger around the collar of his shirt. 'Are you certain you want me to tell you?'

'I'm extremely certain,' I said in a voice that was far stronger than I could have hoped for. 'I'm afraid the police told me very little.'

'Stan's behaviour had changed quite markedly in the weeks before his disappearance.' Gilbert looked at Luke, who gave him a slight nod. 'He didn't tell me, you understand, but I heard from another colleague that Stan intended to move to Brighton.'

'Brighton?' I asked, then blinked rapidly to clear my vision. It was one thing believing something for over a year but quite another to be told that not only were you right, but that your husband planned to move away and leave you behind. Sorrow fought with anger for supremacy in my mind. I was sad our marriage had been a failure, but also angry that I had spent so many years married to a man who ran from his responsibilities.

'Yes.' Gilbert coloured and looked down at the table. 'I'm terribly sorry, Mrs Miller. I thought that perhaps that would come as rather a shock to you. The police didn't mention that to you?'

'They did not,' I confirmed. 'Though I don't know why they would keep such a crucial piece of information from me.'

'Perhaps they thought it would upset you to hear that he planned to move away.'

'I'm more distressed that half of the village where I live think I did something to Stan to prevent him from coming home.' My cheeks burned with embarrassment. 'I would much rather they know the truth.'

'Well, um, yes,' Gilbert stuttered. 'I can see how that would be very difficult for you. However, as far as I am aware, the police could not find any trace of Stan in Brighton, so that lead ran rather cold.'

I took a sip of tea, then lifted my chin. 'Would I be right to think there was another woman involved?'

'I wouldn't know about that,' Gilbert said quickly. Too quickly?

'At this stage, I would rather know.'

'Mrs Miller has been placed in a precarious situation because of her husband's abandonment,' Luke said. 'That is one reason I hoped to find out more today.'

'In what way?'

'Stan's name is the only one on the bank account and the deeds of our home,' I mumbled. The shame of talking about my lack of financial means was awful, but I forced myself to go on. 'I had to take in a lodger so I could meet payments due and cover our bills. It has been a terrible struggle.'

'I'm desperately sorry to hear that.' Gilbert looked up as the waitress arrived with his order. 'If I knew anything more, I would certainly tell you. I personally heard no talk about another woman, only that Stan intended to move to Brighton. I'm afraid that after all this time, I can't even recall who I heard that information from.'

'Might I come to the office with you?' Luke asked. 'Mrs Miller would be ever so grateful.'

Gilbert looked at my face, which I was sure had lost all its colour, and nodded. 'I don't know if it will help, but I would be happy to help in any way that I can.'

I pushed my plate towards Luke. 'I've rather lost my appetite. You eat my scone.'

Luke smiled self-deprecatingly. 'Mrs Miller knows I have a fondness for all baked goods. I'm unable to turn them away.'

'I should imagine the ladies of the village flock to the vicarage with scones, cakes and the like?' Gilbert smiled knowingly.

'I have lived in Westleham only a short time,' Luke replied. 'But that is usually the case when a vicar is new in a parish.'

Gilbert eyed us both curiously, and I could understand why. For a vicar, he certainly knew rather a lot about me and my business. If it looked odd to Gilbert that Luke was keen to involve himself so personally in helping me, he didn't comment on it.

* * *

Later that day, Luke and I retraced our steps to back to Paddington. So far as we were aware, Charles had not left his office building, not even for lunch.

Gilbert had taken Luke to the bank and introduced Luke to different staff members that had employed Stan. The person who had mentioned Stan moving to Brighton had also left the bank. Luke assured me that person was a male colleague, and no one had a forwarding address for him. It was a frustrating dead end, but I did not have the type of money it would take to employ a private investigator to track down either Stan or his colleague.

When Charles Warren finally left his office at the end of the working day, Luke and I walked some distance behind him, but saw nothing unusual. The widower had gone to work and was now returning. If there was a girlfriend, we could see no sign of her.

We travelled towards home separately just in case anyone from the village got on board. Ruby's train home was later than the one I was on, but as we approached Slough it didn't stop me looking out of the window to see if I could see either her or the young man who had approached her earlier that morning. I was determined I would ask her about him when she got home.

When we reached Westleham, I watched Luke get off the train and stride off. Charles Warren disembarked before me with his head down. Although Luke and I were being careful not to be seen, Charles was so lost in his thoughts I didn't think he'd notice if King George himself walked alongside him.

'We can't just follow him down the lane,' I whispered as I caught up to Luke near the ticket office. 'Someone will see us together, or they will catch us following Charles.'

'I shall walk towards the post office and go into the telephone box, as if I am making a call. You just walk home normally. Whichever way he turns, one of us will be behind him.'

'Surely he will go straight home?' I said. 'Look at the poor man. He can hardly keep his head up. He's exhausted.'

We waited out of sight near the train station until Charles and the other travellers reached the end of the path that led to the main street through Westleham. I followed first, and to my amazement, Charles did not turn right towards his own house.

When he reached the church, he walked around the back of the pretty white stone building. With a sinking heart, I realised his destination. Peeking round the wall into the graveyard beyond, I could see Charles crumpled on the ground next to a freshly dug mound of earth.

As they had not yet held the inquest, Alice's body could not be released for burial. (Peter Cameron, who worked as an odd job man as well as the gravedigger, must be particularly low on work that week to have it completed so far in advance.) With nowhere to visit his wife's body, Charles had heartbreakingly chosen to go to what would eventually be her final resting place.

The sound of his sobs reached my ears, and feeling like a voyeur, I hurried back to the path and towards home.

* * *

I had barely reached my gate before Maud came rushing from her home. 'Mrs Miller! Where on earth have you been all day?'

'I... um...' I was about to say I had been shopping in the city. That was clearly a lie, given I did not have any bags with me other than a small handbag. 'I had some things to do in London. To do with Stan... that is... Mr Miller.'

'Excellent. I am pleased to hear it. Oh look, there's the vicar. Cooee!'

I cringed as she hailed Luke in a voice that could stop traffic. He waved across the road. 'Good evening, Mrs Burnett.'

'You must come over to Mrs Miller's house immediately!' Maud cried back.

Luke hurried over and gave me a questioning look. I raised a shoulder to show I did not know what had excited Mrs Burnett.

'Shall we go inside?'

'Yes, we must,' Maud insisted.

'Is something wrong?' I fumbled in my bag for my door key. It had felt quite odd that morning to lock my door, but after Alice's death, I had decided that I should be more careful. Stan would be so proud of me.

'Yes,' Maud said urgently. 'Terribly wrong.'

Eventually, I found the key, unlocked the door and pushed it open. Lizzie came bounding down the hall to greet us. Not used to being on her own all day, and with three people all arriving at the same time, she was giddy with excitement.

'I should take her outside,' I said.

'Mrs Miller,' Maud said sharply. 'I insist you sit down at the kitchen table with the vicar while I explain what has been going on in your absence.'

Heat rose to my cheeks. Had we been spotted despite our care? Had the bishop visited the village to castigate Luke for his lax morals? I flopped into a chair without putting the kettle on to boil. I had no wish to prolong Mrs Burnett's stay.

'What is wrong, Mrs Burnett?' Luke asked calmly. How could he be so relaxed when I felt as though my entire world was about to tumble around my head?

'It's Mrs Harrington.' Maud paused dramatically.

'Yes?'

'She's dead.'

'Dead?' I sat up straight and looked at Luke. His face mirrored the shock I was certain showed on my own.

'Yes,' Maud confirmed. 'Quite dead.'

'What a terrible tragedy.' Luke shook his head. For once, his composure slipped and his gaze flittered around the kitchen as though he was searching for something appropriate to say before landing on Mrs Burnett. 'Mr Harrington must be devastated. Goodness me, those poor children.'

'Mrs Harrington's mother has already been and taken the children to stay with her. Apparently, Mr Harrington was quite inconsolable.' Maud revelled in her role of imparting her knowledge to us.

'Do we know what happened?'

'Well, I'm not one to spread gossip, as you know' – Maud leaned forward, seemingly completely unaware of the irony of her statement – 'but I heard it from Mrs Felton who, as is well known, is good friends with the doctor's cleaner. Evidently, she was poisoned with the sachets the doctor gives her to help her sleep. That rather attractive detective has questioned Doctor Briggs all afternoon.'

'Poison?' I asked sharply.

'What a dreadful state of affairs,' Luke said. Slowly, he looked between me and Mrs Burnett as though he was struggling to process the facts as Maud was giving them to us.

'You've missed all the action,' Maud crowed as though the village was a cinema and we had popped out during the best bit of the film.

'Could it be possible that Mrs Harrington has been poisoned by the same method as Mrs Warren?'

'Two poisonings suggest it's more likely than not.' My first emotion was relief. If Elsie died in the same way as Alice, wouldn't that mean I was no longer a suspect? Shame flooded through me as the reality of the situation came hard on the heels of my own self-interests.

'I should get along to the Harringtons' home immediately.' Luke got to his feet and hurried out of the house.

'I can't stay either, Mrs Miller.' Maud moved faster than a woman her age had any right to.

I walked mechanically to the back door to let Lizzie out. I sat on the back step as my dog ran joyfully around the garden, stopping every couple of steps to sniff a patch of grass.

What did the news mean? Mrs Warren and Mrs Harrington both dead – seemingly both poisoned. Was there a prolific murderer in the village and, if so, who would be next?

9

I had barely enough time to contemplate the new incident before a rather ominous pounding started on my front door. There was no doubt in my mind that it would be Detective Inspector Robertson, demanding to know my alibi for the day.

Indecision slowed my feet as I left Lizzie in the garden and walked to the front of the house. I opened the door, and my fears were realised. The detective stood on my doorstep with two uniformed constables.

'Good evening, Inspector.'

'Mrs Miller.' He raised his hat in greeting. 'May we come in?'

I nodded and stood back to allow them entrance. Keeping my head down, I closed the door behind them. There was no need to look along the street to know that I was, once again, the talk of the village. For months after Stan's disappearance, I had been an oddity in the village. Wives in quaint little English villages were not suddenly abandoned by their husband. Neither did they then turn their lawn into a vegetable patch. While it was acceptable I earned my living from the land during the war, it was frowned upon during peacetime. I longed to be anonymous and instantly forgettable as I'd been during my marriage to Stan.

Leading the way through to the parlour, I sat on my usual chair near the window. 'How can I help you?'

It was a ridiculous question. The reason he was here, with two officers in uniform, was clear. He was going to arrest me. Trying not to show how afraid I was, I folded my hands in my lap to stop them from trembling.

'Where have you been all day?'

'Shopping in London.' The lie automatically fell from my lips.

'Mrs Miller,' the detective said with exaggerating patience. 'I watched you walk down the lane, including a strange detour to the back of the church, then on to your cottage. You were not carrying any shopping bags.'

'I found nothing I wanted to buy.'

He raised an eyebrow. 'There was nothing in any of the shops in London that was to your liking?'

'That isn't quite what I said,' I replied, my confidence returning as my lie took shape. 'I liked lots of things, but I'm afraid I couldn't afford the price.'

'You're telling me you caught a train all the way to London to look at things you could not pay for?'

'Yes, that's exactly it.'

'Perhaps you can remember the names of some of the shops where you looked at things you couldn't buy?' His sharp tone told me the detective wasn't an idiot. One constable sniggered, and I wished I was clever enough to think of a more plausible reason to be out all day.

I couldn't admit to being with the vicar all day. It really wasn't appropriate. The last thing I wanted was to involve him any more than he already was in the mess I was in. Neither did I want to air my humiliation at finding out Stan planned to leave me and move to Brighton.

'I'm sorry, no.' I smiled to cover my growing unease. 'I was enjoying browsing so much I paid no attention to the names of the shops I went into.'

'That leaves you in a troublesome situation, Mrs Miller.'

'It does? How so?'

'While you have been gone, there has been another murder in the village.'

If he had watched me walk down the lane and follow Charles Warren to the church, he certainly knew that Maud had paid me a visit as soon as I returned. I switched to the truth. 'I have heard the terrible news.'

'As an intelligent woman, I am sure you know I must ask everyone for their alibi. Especially someone like you who, I am told, was verbally attacked by Mrs Harrington on Saturday.'

'Surely that gives her a motive to kill *me*.'

'That's an excellent point' – he inclined his head, but before I could allow myself that small victory, his eyes flashed – 'if you were dead and Mrs Harrington was the woman being questioned.'

'Yes, I can see that.' I stood up. 'I do apologise. Where are my manners? Shall I make tea? Who would—'

'Sit down, Mrs Miller.'

I flopped into my chair, and a prickle of dread danced all the way up my spine, leaving the hairs on the back of my neck standing on end. 'I think we have established you have no alibi for today. Perhaps you can explain to me how Mrs Harrington came to have a bottle of your plum gin on her bedside table?'

I blinked. Plum Gin? No alibi?

Well, that wasn't entirely true. I *did* have an alibi, I just didn't want to embarrass Luke or put him into a difficult situation by admitting that we had spent the day together in London. Even though we had gone on a perfectly valid mission, I wanted to protect the vicar's reputation as well as my own. Surely I could explain to the detective satisfactorily why I couldn't have killed Elsie without involving Luke? I knew better than most how it felt to have your reputation be the talk of the village. I desperately didn't want the vicar to suffer the same shame.

And as for the gin, my mind raced. I had donated quite a few bottles to the village show and, of course, Joe Noble sold them at the pub. It seemed churlish to draw attention to Joe, given he'd said Elsie was fond a drink. 'Perhaps she picked one up after the show.'

'Why would she do that after watching Mrs Warren die?'

'If she had bought it somewhere prior to the show, why would she keep it if she thought it was connected to Mrs Warren's death?' I lifted my chin. 'Am I to presume that the cause of death has something to do with my plum gin? I was told it was her sleeping powder.'

'We assumed at first the glass of clear liquid next to her bed contained water, and that she had used it to mix with her sleeping draught. Then I found the bottle of gin.'

'So it could still be water in the glass?' I narrowed my eyes as anger took over from fear. 'Why are you here questioning me about my gin when you don't know for sure what killed her?'

'I'm sure you understand the need for us to gather evidence at this early stage. The glass in Mrs Harrington's house, as well as the one used by Mrs Warren, will be analysed for poison.'

'This is ridiculous!' The swirling maelstrom of emotions I had tried to keep inside all day burst free. 'How dare you suggest my gin has anything to do with either death? Lots of people drank my plum gin at the show and they suffered no ill effects. As for Mrs Harrington having a bottle near her bed, that could have once contained my gin, but who is to say what has since been put in it? You're aware Mrs Harrington did not like me. So how, please tell me, do you think I got into her house, let alone her bedroom, to put the poison into the bottle?'

'As I said, we are in the early stages of gathering evidence.' His voice was calm and reasoned, which only frustrated me further.

'Instead of sitting here insulting me and my plum gin, why don't you go over the road and speak to George Felton?' I snapped. 'You received the telephone message I left for you, I presume?'

'What message?'

'For goodness' sake,' I exploded. 'I should not have to do your job for you.'

'Can you explain?' Brown eyes flicked between me and the constables standing to his left. The force with which he gripped the arm of the chair told me he was close to losing his temper. I hoped it was with his colleagues and not with me. There was a clear thread of steel running through him that both intrigued and terrified me in equal measures.

'The message I left for you was regarding evidence I uncovered about George Felton who lives opposite to me.' I nodded through the window to my left. 'I believe he is the person responsible for vandalising gardens in the village.'

'With all due respect, Mrs Miller' – Detective Inspector Robertson's mouth twitched as though he was trying hard not to laugh at me – 'we are investigating two murders. Vandalism doesn't really interest us at the moment.'

'Well, it should, and I shall show you why.' I grabbed my knitting basket from next to my chair and delved into the bottom, where I'd hidden the notes from the committee meeting implicating George. Although I had locked my door, I didn't want to leave anything to chance, and so had hidden the papers in a place

I hoped no one would think of looking. 'I visited Mrs Leaming the day after the show to see who would have won prizes. I was surprised to see George's name as a winner for his broad beans because he had complained earlier this year that those particular crops had been destroyed by a vandal.'

The detective leaned forward, his attention clearly piqued. 'Go on.'

'Mr Warren offered me the committee papers kept by his wife. When I searched for the May meeting, I found it was indeed his broad beans George claimed were destroyed.'

'Would Mrs Warren have been aware of that?'

'She had the document proving his lie in her house. I recalled his claim, so she may have done too. Perhaps she spoke to George and threatened to reveal his lie at the show and give the prize to someone else, and so he killed her before she could. I wouldn't know about that. As you've already pointed out, it's *your* job to investigate the important crimes.'

He blinked as my intended barb hit its mark. 'Does George have a connection to Mrs Harrington that you're aware of?'

'He is the Harringtons' gardener. Although that is an outside job, I'm sure he has access to the house. If village rumours are true that Mrs Harrington is fond of a drink, that would explain the gin next to her bed. Perhaps George was aware of her predilection for alcohol and knew he would have ample opportunities to kill her.'

'What motive would he have for killing her?'

'I don't know, Inspector. Perhaps you can find his motive without any help from me?'

His face broke out into a grin, which heightened his good looks. 'I shall look into Mr Felton.' He pointed a finger at me. 'But you're not off the hook yet though.'

After I had shown the police out, I went back to the garden.

Lizzie ran to me and nuzzled my hand. Whilst I was relieved I had avoided admitting I'd spent the day with the vicar, I was still concerned that someone seemed to be using my plum gin to poison villagers. It was disconcerting to think that someone hated me so much they were happy to frame me for two murders.

'I know, girl.' I stroked her head. 'Yet another person is dead with my gin nearby. What an almighty mess.'

* * *

A short time later, Ruby came crashing into the kitchen. 'Martha! You'll never believe it! I've just seen George Felton being carted off in a *police car*!'

'Have you heard the other news?'

'About horrid Harrington?'

'Ruby!'

She spread her hands wide. 'Well, she was rather ghastly, Martha.'

'She was very unkind to me,' I agreed, 'but I'm certain she didn't deserve to die.'

'Who knows? Maybe she did something the killer didn't like, and he bumped her off.'

'He?'

'It almost always is, isn't it?'

'Yes, I suppose it is.' I opened the fridge. 'I'm afraid it's only salad tonight, Ruby. I haven't had a chance to cook anything since I got back from the city.'

She shrugged. 'I don't mind. It's jolly hot, and I'm not awfully hungry.'

'Can I ask you something?'

'You can ask me whatever you like, Martha, but I can't say that I'll answer until I know what you're asking.'

I took a breath and rushed ahead before I could change my mind and ask something innocuous. 'Who was that man I saw you with this morning?'

Guilt filled eyes looked at me before she looked down at her nails. 'Which man?'

'The one at Slough station. I saw him grab hold of your arm.' I held my breath. Our relationship was improving, and I didn't want my question to cause Ruby to be upset with me, but I couldn't stop myself from asking. I hadn't liked the way he had touched her.

'Oh, him.' She kicked off her shoes. 'He's no one.'

'I didn't like the look of him.'

'He's mostly harmless.'

'Mostly? Ruby, I—'

'Please don't worry about me. I have the situation under control.' She picked up her shoes and headed to the door. 'I'm going to go up and change. Honestly, Martha, everything is fine.'

Her reluctance to even tell me the man's name told me that things were not 'fine'. I could only hope that Ruby knew what she was doing.

* * *

The next day, I walked down to the pub shortly before it opened. I wanted to find out from Joe Noble what he had done with the leftover bottles after the show. There must have been some since it ended so abruptly.

I went around to the back. Florence was hanging washing out in the small yard. 'Oh, Mrs Miller, good morning.'

'Good morning, Florence. I wonder if I might have a word with your father, please?'

'You haven't come to tell him about... you know? My secret?'

'Of course not,' I reassured her. 'I told you I wouldn't.'

'I'll fetch him.' She smiled, but paused at the doorstep. 'Mother won't like him chatting when he should be busy getting the pub ready.'

'I'll be quick, I promise.'

Joe came outside with his daughter. 'What is it, Mrs Miller? I'm very busy.'

'When did you last have a visit from the brewery?' I had thought all night about how best to broach the subject of illegal alcohol sales with Mr Noble and, in the end had decided to be direct.

His face reddened. 'Not for a while.'

'Do you keep the cellar locked when they come to inspect your pub?' I rubbed my chin. 'Or is it their pub? I'm never quite sure how these things work.'

'Now, Mrs Miller,' Joe said placatingly. 'I have a feeling you know precisely how things work with the brewery. Why don't you spit out the reason for your visit?'

'Despite what you have led me to believe, the brewery has not given you permission to sell my bottles of gin, have they?'

'What makes you say that?'

'If they knew, then you surely would have told the detective that the reason there was a bottle of my gin in Mrs Harrington's bedroom was because you had sold her it. That's also the reason you were very certain that she likes a drink, isn't it? Because you sell my gin to her.'

'I'm sure we can come to some sort of arrangement.' He lowered his voice, his tone no longer confident but wheedling and a little whiny. 'There's no need for anyone else to know about this. Especially the wife.'

'You will have to make it worth my while.' I folded my arms. 'If the brewery has not been taking their cut all these months, then you have been woefully underpaying me and pocketing the profits yourself.'

'It isn't that simple.'

'Then make it that simple,' I said. 'You don't want me to speak to the inspector and explain to him how Mrs Harrington got hold of a bottle of my gin, do you? Unless, of course, you poisoned it before you sold her it.'

'What motive do I have for killing Mrs Harrington?' he asked indignantly, shock registering on his face at my sudden accusation.

I spread my hands wide. 'What reason do I have?'

'Everyone heard how mean she was to you after Mrs Warren died.'

'If I killed everyone who has been rude to me at one time or another, there would be no one left in this village,' I retorted.

He laughed. 'True enough. People are rather unkind to you, and all because your husband took up with a fancy woman.'

'What do you know about that?' I asked sharply.

'I overheard the coppers talking about it.' He shuffled his feet. 'The detective fellow apparently said he thought the villagers were vindictive, suggesting you'd killed Stan when it was clear—'

I held up a hand. 'I think once was enough. I don't want to hear it again.'

'Sorry.' He hung his head. 'For what it's worth, your husband was a rude, stuffy man who wouldn't know a good thing if it hit him in the face.'

'Thank you, Mr Noble. That's very sweet.' I smiled, pleasantly surprised at the publican's words. Had I been so preoccupied with my own disappointment at Stan's desertion that I hadn't noticed not all villagers felt the same as Ada Garrett? 'Now, what are we to do about the money you owe me?'

'You appreciate the situation I'm in with the missus?'

'You appreciate the situation I'm in with money?' I put a hand on my hip. 'I don't want to make things awkward for you, but the entire village knows how difficult things have been for me financially. Let me propose a deal.'

'A deal?' he sounded doubtful, but my mind was made up. I could see a way to help deflect the detective's suspicion off me as well as get the money Joe owed me.

'I will ensure the detective doesn't tell the brewery about your little money-making scheme.'

'And in return?'

'You will tell him you provided Mrs Harrington with the bottle of gin, and you will pay me what you owe. Today.'

'That sounds rather like blackmail.' He rubbed a hand over his sparse hair. 'I'm not sure I like that.'

'Well, I know I don't like you taking advantage of my good nature. I *trusted* you when you told me the brewery agreed to you selling my gin in your pub. I was *grateful!*'

'I'll see what I can—'

'Not good enough,' I snapped. 'Stop taking advantage of me, otherwise I will go to the brewery myself.'

I marched off. I think Ruby would be proud of me. Little mousey Martha Miller was learning how to stand up for herself!

I hoped Joe would come good with the money because I was going to suggest to Ruby that we went into the city together this weekend to watch a film.

My only slight fear was, what if Joe had killed both women? If so, then I had just angered a killer. I shook my head. That was nonsense. Joe had no reason to kill Alice and Elsie – or did he?

10

After lunch, I worked in my neglected garden, despite the stifling heat of the beautiful summer day. Lizzie lay in the shade of my enormous apple tree.

'It's impossible to work out.' I pulled at a particularly stubborn weed growing in the middle of my neat row of beetroot plants. 'I don't think George killed them. I know the police have arrested him, and I can obviously understand why. But even after he was so aggressive towards me, I still don't think it fits.'

Lizzie half opened one eye, as though she could sense me looking over at her. She thumped her tail and closed her eyes again.

'You're no help. All you do is lie there sleeping. What I need is for someone to go through everything that I know with me. Maybe if we put our heads together, we can come up with the answer.'

'Mrs Miller.' Maud's head popped up over the hedge separating our gardens. 'You do know that dog will never answer you, don't you?'

I swallowed my embarrassment. 'I like talking to her.'

'You should spend more time talking to people.' Maud pointed a finger at me. 'Did you sort things out in the city? With your husband? You really should make more of an effort to dress nicely. Like you did for the show. Taking care of one's appearance is certainly an effective way to capture a man.'

'I've never been one to spend hours in front of the mirror,' I said. 'And I still managed to find myself a man.'

'And just look at how that turned out.'

I wanted to argue, be a loyal wife and say something praising Stan. Sadly, it was too hard to think of anything positive to say about him or our marriage.

'I saw the way the vicar was looking at you on Saturday. Who would have thought that under those awful clothes you usually wear you would have such good legs?'

I wasn't sure of an appropriate response. Of course, I knew Maud noticed absolutely everything. She missed nothing. Still, it felt jolly uncomfortable that she should notice my figure so thoroughly.

'Thank you. How very kind of you to say.' I swept out an arm across my garden. 'I really should get on.'

'Don't let me stop you.' But Maud did not disappear back into her own garden as I hoped. 'Now, what did the lovely vicar find out when he went into London yesterday?'

I had to be careful about what I told her. She would repeat everything I said, probably with embellishments, to everyone in the village, whether or not they cared about me and my marriage.

'Nothing very significant,' I said. 'There is some suggestion that Stan may have moved to live in the Brighton area. Apparently, the police already had that information and could not verify it. So I'm afraid I'm not any further on.'

'Then you must track him down,' she said fervently. 'You can't stop now. You absolutely must find out where he is, then you can serve him with divorce papers.'

'I'm afraid it's not that easy. In order for me to divorce Stan, I have to prove that he has committed adultery. Either that, or we must have been separated for three years.' I stared at her in horror. Why was I telling her all this? 'And I'm not even sure that is what I want to do.'

'Stuff and nonsense! Why on earth would you want to remain tied to that man?'

'We were married in a church,' I said defensively. 'I believe wholeheartedly in the institution of marriage.'

'I couldn't agree more,' Maud said. 'But only when one is married to the correct person. I think you and the new vicar would make a very attractive couple.'

'Mrs Burnett! Even if the vicar was interested in me, which I sincerely doubt, then the church would surely have something to say about any potential relationship.' We had moved way past what I felt comfortable talking about with my neighbour. I did not know how she would report this conversation to the rest of the village. But I was certain it would contain inaccuracies and flourishes that Maud would add to make it more salacious.

I really needed to find myself some real friends so I didn't end up telling my dog – and my nosy neighbour – everything about my life.

* * *

Later that evening, Ruby arrived home from work with an unexpected guest.

'Good evening, Mrs Miller. I wanted to come and let you know where we are with the investigation,' Detective Inspector Robertson said as I opened the door.

'What you mean is whether you are still following the ridiculous theory that my sister killed Alice and Elsie.' Ruby put one hand on her hip and faced the detective across the small entranceway.

'Ruby, can we at least let the detective inside to talk about this?'

'Not if he is going to continue with his ridiculous accusations against you.'

'Your sister has refused to give me an alibi for the day Elsie Harrington was murdered, Miss Andrews.'

'Oh, but that's easy.' As the detective's gaze swung to Ruby, I shook my head rapidly and mouthed the word 'no'. Of course, my sister completely ignored my frantic gesturing. 'Martha was in London all day with the vicar.'

'Why didn't you just say so?' He looked at me, anger clouding his handsome face. Ruby pivoted and added her puzzled stare to that of the detective.

'I'm a married woman,' I said defensively. 'If people were to find out I had gone to London with the vicar, he would be the victim of an endless stream of gossip.'

'Mrs Miller,' the detective said with exaggerated patience, 'it may have escaped your notice, but I am not "people". I am a police detective. I'm not in the habit of learning information about suspects in my enquiries and then repeating it to all and sundry.'

'Of course, yes.' I looked down at the floor. 'I can see that. At the time, Luke, that is the vicar, had spoken to some of Stan's work colleagues. I had found out some distressing news and perhaps that caused me to be rather secretive when you came to the house to question me following Elsie's death.'

'What distressing news might that be?'

He spoke carefully, but he had a very expressive face. There was no doubt he was already aware of the information I had learned. It was just as obvious that he was rather taken by my sister. That was clear in the very studious way he avoided looking at her. Yet every time she spoke, the very tips of his ears turned slightly pink.

'Apparently Stan made plans to move to Brighton.'

'Yes, I read that in the files.'

'Why were you reading the file about my husband's disappearance?' I tried to keep the unhappiness from my tone. It was all so humiliating.

'Yes, why would you do that?' Ruby said, causing the detective's ears to flare again. 'And more to the point, why did you not share that knowledge with my sister?'

Detective Inspector Robertson removed his hat and gestured with it towards the parlour door. 'Perhaps we might sit down?'

'I would very much like to hear what you have to say.' Ruby marched towards the parlour, stopped in the doorway, then turned and looked at the detective over her shoulder.

He turned redder than the telephone box outside the post office. 'Where should I... I mean...'

'Detective?' Oh, how I envied Ruby's ability to render a man practically speechless.

'My hat.' He lifted it slightly, as if I was in any doubt about what he was talking about.

I pointed at the hatstand opposite the grandfather clock in the hallway. 'You may leave your hat and your jacket on there.'

'Of course.'

'Can I get you a glass of water? You look rather flushed.' It wasn't very kind of me to tease the detective, but after the way he had treated me – as though I was a suspect in not one but two murder cases – I couldn't help myself. Not to mention how awful it was having to go over Stan's desertion yet again.

'Thank you,' he said, seeming to pull himself together. 'That would be very kind.'

I went through to the kitchen, took out a jug of lemonade and placed it on the tray together with three glasses. When I walked into the parlour, I don't know who looked more awkward – my sister, who was perched awkwardly in my usual seat, or the detective, who stared resolutely ahead as though one glance at Ruby would cause him to spontaneously combust.

'I have lemonade, made earlier and fresh out of the refrigerator.' The words were extremely needless, given that any fool could see what I had carried through. I put the tray on the table in front of the detective. 'Please help yourself.'

'My sister makes the best lemonade,' Ruby bragged. 'I suppose you will need one of us to take a drink first to make sure she hasn't poisoned it?'

'That will not be necessary,' he said stiffly. 'I'm sure it's quite lovely.'

'You said you came here specifically to tell me something?' I asked.

'Yes, I thought you would like to know that you were correct about George Felton. He has confessed to being the village vandal.'

A small thrill rippled its way up my spine. My investigation was successful – now to uncover the murderer!

'What have you charged him with?'

'Criminal damage.' The detective frowned. 'I don't expect that he will get a particularly onerous sentence. Probably a fine and some sort of community service.'

'I think the shame of what he has done will be far greater than any criminal sanctions.'

'Have you released the lunatic?' Ruby asked angrily.

'Mr Felton is now back at home with his wife, yes.'

Ruby leaned forward in her chair and twisted round to look at the detective. 'What are you doing to keep the women of this village safe?'

'From Mr Felton?'

'Of course from Mr Felton,' she snapped.

'Mr Felton has an alibi for both deaths.'

'And you believe what he says?'

'We have independent witnesses to corroborate what Mr Felton has told us.'

'Can you share those alibis with us?' I asked. Was the detective not aware that people frequently lied to get themselves out of a difficult situation?

'In a village such as this one, I do not see that keeping details of Mr Felton's alibi private will do any good. I'm certain that most of the village already know that Mr Felton had not entered the marquee before Mrs Warren's death. Many witnesses attest to the fact he spent all day with his vegetables and a continuous supply of cold beer. On the morning of Mrs Harrington's death, he was not in the village but had gone to visit old army friends in Slough. We have taken several statements that confirm his attendance at their monthly reunion lunch.'

Ruby sat back in the chair. 'Then we are right back to where we started?'

'I didn't think George had killed anyone, anyway.'

'Really, Mrs Miller? Why not?'

'I think the killer is a sly, rather clever person. George is neither. He is a very angry man and not clever enough to pull off what I think are well-thought-out murders.'

'What makes you say they are well thought out?'

'Simple,' I said, as though the answer was obvious – because, to me, it was. 'We don't have one clue who the person is, not one.

That rather suggests to me the killer is very sneaky and incredibly careful.'

Detective Inspector Robertson drained his lemonade and folded his arms across his chest. 'I *will* find the perpetrator. You can be sure of that. No matter how clever, sneaky, or careful he or she is.'

* * *

Ten minutes after the detective left, there was another knock at the door. Ruby got to her feet, but I motioned her to sit back down. 'I'll get it. You've had a busy day at work. Go get changed and I'll get supper on the table. Whoever it is will have to speak to me while I prepare our meal.'

I opened the door, expecting it to be Maud, wanting to know what the detective told me. Instead, it was Luke. 'Good evening, Vicar.'

'Did I see Detective Inspector Robertson leaving a few moments ago?'

'I think your gossip radar is as finely honed as Mrs Burnett's.'

He smiled. 'Surely not?'

'You had better come in.'

'If you're sure I'm not disturbing you?'

'Come through to the kitchen. I was just about to start supper for Ruby and me. Can I interest you in a vegetable omelette?'

'That's very kind.' He wrinkled his nose in distaste. 'Unfortunately, Mrs Felton has left some sort of casserole for me. I must make an attempt to eat it, otherwise I fear she will report me to the bishop.'

'Surely not?'

'She made a comment about me not eating her food and went

on to say that if her efforts were not up to my standard, perhaps I needed to speak to the bishop about replacing her.'

'Oh dear.' I put my apron over my head and tied it loosely behind my back. 'So now you feel as though you have to eat everything that she puts before you?'

'I'm new here. Last thing I want is for the bishop to come to Westleham because he thinks there is something wrong in the parish.'

'I think the bishop would be very surprised if he knew the goings-on here recently.' Pulling out a chopping board, I gathered peppers, shallots, tomatoes and a courgette from the refrigerator. I then took down the bowl containing fresh eggs from the cupboard. 'I don't have much, but I do have more than enough fresh eggs and vegetables to go around. Are you sure you won't change your mind?'

'No, I fear I must eat Mrs Felton's offering.' Luke pulled a face. 'If I am honest, I was so intrigued to know what the detective wanted, supper went completely out of my mind. Do you know anything more about our little village mystery?'

I chopped into a red pepper and removed the seeds with a spoon. 'Funnily enough, this afternoon, before DI Robertson popped in, I was hoping to go through what I knew about Alice and Elsie's deaths. I'm glad you're here because, perhaps, if we put our heads together, we can work out what we are missing.'

'What is the first thing that puzzles you?'

'Mrs Harrington's behaviour after Alice died. We have never been friends, but her behaviour towards me was very peculiar. She is normally a very strait-laced kind of lady, not one to lose control, especially in public. I could barely believe it when she called Ruby and I trollops. What a word to use!'

'We know why she behaved that way, though, don't we?' Luke asked. 'It is because she had been drinking excessively. Unfortunately, many people act badly when they have had too much alcohol.'

'We should exercise caution believing everything we have been told. But that part seems factually correct. Joe Noble has admitted Mrs Harrington bought alcohol from him on the quiet. She also had a bottle of gin in her bedroom – I don't know of anyone who doesn't have a strong dependency on alcohol who'd keep spirits upstairs in their house.'

'What about Charles Warren? He seemed so incredibly and genuinely distraught over Alice's death, but can we really cross him out as a suspect when he is going to come into such a large sum of money?'

'I didn't tell you what happened when I followed him from the train on Tuesday. He went directly to the graveyard and sobbed over Alice's grave.'

'But there is no grave there,' Luke protested. 'Just a hole until the coroner releases her body for burial.'

'I know. That was what made it so much more tragic. Alice wasn't even there, but yet poor Mr Warren seemed to need somewhere to mourn.'

'Poor man.' Luke paused, looking down at the table, before continuing. 'I have had some thoughts about Mrs Leaming. You mentioned there was rather a lot of furniture and animals in her home. I went to university with a chap who now works as a vet. Perhaps I could call him and have him visit Mrs Leaming on some pretext or other?'

I raised an eyebrow. 'I'm not sure what that would achieve. We know she's acting very strangely, but she was extremely friendly towards me following Alice's death. I don't know that your friend could uncover the reason for her abrupt mood change.'

'He might be able to get some information out of her, with

him being a stranger. He's a very personable fellow. Is it worth a
try at least?'

'I think *you* should visit her,' I said. 'It wouldn't look so odd.
You said you needed to visit all of your parishioners.'

'All right.' He nodded. 'I can see your point. I shall give it a go.
Would you consider speaking to Ernest Harrington? He gave me
very short shrift when he found me talking to Elsie the other day.'

'Do you think he would be any more keen to speak to me?'

'It might be that he's the sort of man who reacts better to a
woman.' He lifted a shoulder at my doubtful expression. 'I think
we should try everything we can, even if it seems outlandish.
Speaking of which, it's about time I went to the local pub.'

'I didn't know you were fond of a tipple, Vicar,' I said.

Thinking about it, there was a lot I didn't know about him. I
wanted to know more. He had been such a comfort to me over the
last few days. What on earth would I have done without him
believing in me so thoroughly? Of course, Ruby knew I couldn't
possibly have been involved in Alice and Elsie's death, but she
was my sister. It was practically in the family rule book she had to
stick up for me. Luke, however, was new to the village and there
was no reason for him to be on my side. Yet he was.

Warmth spread through my stomach at the prospect of our
friendship deepening. My shattered self-confidence was
improving almost daily as I realised not everyone blamed me for
the breakdown of my marriage.

'I don't mind the odd pint of beer or a tot of brandy on special
occasions. I haven't yet met Joe Noble, but I shall remedy that this
evening.'

Looking up from the chopping board, I saw Luke's raised
eyebrow and realised his trip to the pub was nothing to do with
wanting to sample its wares. 'Ah. I see your plan. You are going to
the pub to find out what you can from Joe. We really need to

know if there is any reason he might have killed Alice. Was there something that she knew about him? We know he was selling alcohol without the brewery's knowledge. Could Alice have found out about that? Was she threatening him?'

'We have so many more questions than answers. Perhaps if we find some answers, we will be closer to finding out who the murderer is.'

'I suppose that after what you told me about Mrs Garrett, I must talk to her and clear the air.'

He looked thoughtful for a moment. 'I should think that having a lady like Mrs Garrett on your side would be a lot more beneficial than having her as an enemy.'

'Not to mention she is the queen of gossip in this village. There isn't a thing that goes on that she doesn't know about. Perhaps I should do my best to make a friend of her, despite our past differences.'

'I think that's an excellent idea.'

'Unless it turns out she is the murderer, of course.'

'Do you really think she might be?'

I cracked eggs into a jug and whisked them briskly with a fork. 'I don't really want to rule anyone out unless we can categorically prove it wasn't them.'

'Do we trust what Detective Inspector Robertson said about George being innocent?'

'I don't see how it matters where he was on the morning of the second murder.' I dropped the fork into the sink. 'Where he was immediately prior to her death doesn't matter. He could have added the poison to the bottle at any time.'

'I see what you mean.' Luke gazed at me thoughtfully. 'We can only rule him out at the actual time of her death, but he did not need to be present for the poison to work.'

'Unless, of course, she was as much of a drinker as Joe Noble says and the only time it could have been added was directly before she poured herself a drink. If the poison was present in the bottle when she purchased it, she would have died when taking her first drink.'

'What if she didn't make the drink herself?'

'Gosh, we haven't considered that, have we?'

'Surely the police have? Though Alice didn't make her own drink either.'

I abandoned the chopped vegetables and sat at the table opposite Luke. 'We shouldn't suspect Florence though, surely?'

'Did she make the drinks?'

'I didn't ask,' I admitted. 'I simply presumed she did.'

'What if she didn't?' he asked quietly. 'That would rather change everything, wouldn't it?'

I twisted my hands in my apron. 'We already knew it could have been anyone, but until now, I assumed the murderer added the poison to the bottle.'

'Me too.' His mouth twisted in consternation. 'If they added the poison to an individual glass, that makes things even more complicated.'

'It means the murderer couldn't know who was going to take the glass.'

'So it follows Alice might not have been the intended victim.'

'That changes everything.' I looked at Luke in horror. 'It would mean someone is simply poisoning random villagers for no reason whatsoever.'

I shuddered. It was too horrible to contemplate.

Why would anyone do that in our sleepy little village?

11

The following morning, I had barely finished washing the breakfast dishes when there was a knock on the door. I couldn't think who would call so early. My heart hammered a staccato rhythm in my chest. Had someone else died? What had my life become that wondering if there had been another death was my first thought?

Reluctantly, I left the kitchen and walked through the hall to the front door. I took a deep breath to fortify myself. Whoever was on the other side of the door lifted the knocker and pounded it against the stopper. Jumping back from the door, I startled Lizzie, who began barking.

I grabbed her collar. 'Shush, it's fine.'

Without allowing myself to procrastinate any further, I yanked open the door, my nerves shredded and my hands shaking.

'Good morning, Mrs Miller.' Margaret Leaming looked down at Lizzie with a look of obvious distaste. 'Is that animal dangerous?'

Certainly not and, furthermore, she doesn't use my house as her toilet either!

I kept my initial thoughts to myself. 'Of course not.'

'Are you going to invite me inside, dear?'

I stepped back from the door. Today, Mrs Leaming was back to her normal self. The bedraggled creature who answered the door to me on Sunday afternoon was gone.

'Please, come inside.' Usually I took visitors into the kitchen. Like all the other villagers, I mainly reserved my parlour for relaxing in an evening or for important guests. Given the way Margaret was looking at Lizzie, I'd rather leave my beloved dog in the kitchen than have her anywhere near the committee secretary.

As soon as Margaret's bottom hit the green striped sofa, she got straight to the point. 'Mrs Miller, as the acting chair of the committee, I am letting you know I am tendering my resignation as the secretary.'

She slapped an envelope down on the table in front of her. I hovered near the door, wondering whether I should make tea or if the conversation was over as far as Mrs Leaming was concerned. I couldn't let her leave before I'd asked her more questions, so I ushered Lizzie into the kitchen and closed the parlour door behind me.

Standing next to the fireplace, I faced Margaret. 'Is there anything I can do to get you to reconsider?'

'There is not.' Margaret folded her arms across her chest. 'People are dying, Mrs Miller. Not only am I resigning as secretary, but I also intend to leave this village. If I don't, perhaps I will be the next person poisoned by some madman.'

To my horror, Margaret burst into noisy sobs. I moved to her side and patted her shoulder awkwardly. 'There, there. I'm sure you're not in danger.'

I wasn't sure of anything of the sort. If we didn't know the motive of the poisoner, how could any of us possibly know who might be targeted next?

Margaret dug into a handbag the size of a small travelling case and eventually extracted a crumpled handkerchief.

'Oh, Mrs Miller. We could both be in his sights right at this moment. Mrs Warren was killed in front of the whole village and Mrs Harrington in her own home. None of us are safe. That is to say, none of us women are safe. It appears the men of the village have nothing to worry about.'

Other than the death of their wives, of course, but I didn't say that. In the circumstances, I didn't think it would be very helpful.

'And you're so afraid you intend to move out of the village?'

'At the earliest opportunity,' she confirmed. 'I'm afraid to eat or drink anything. Sleeping is now a luxury I can't afford. I'm too afraid I won't wake up.'

'You seemed extremely upset when I saw you on Sunday,' I said, watching her face closely to gauge her reaction.

'I think I was in shock when I spoke to you at the show. Afterwards, when what happened hit me, I struggled to hold myself together. I don't mind admitting, Mrs Miller, this entire business has been the very worst thing that has ever happened to me.'

Worse than losing her husband? I hadn't fallen to pieces when Stan disappeared, but surely most wives in a similar situation would think that was the most difficult time in their lives?

'We will be terribly sorry to lose you in the village, Mrs Leaming.' She blew her nose noisily, and I was thankful to see her tears had stopped. 'You are such an efficient secretary.'

I was a horrible person. Although it was nice to be praised for a job well done, it wasn't very flattering that the only thing I could suggest that Mrs Leaming would be missed for was her work as the committee secretary.

'That's very kind of you to say.' She sniffed and dropped her handkerchief back into her handbag.

I needed to ask her more questions before I could let her go. I tried to remember the things we wanted to ask. Not for the first time, I wished I used a notebook during my conversation with Luke. Or had a memory that worked. Either would be useful right now.

'Where will you go?' I walked over to the chair next to the window and sat down.

'I have a house in Cornwall.'

'Really? How lovely.'

Margaret flushed and looked down at her handbag. 'I inherited it.'

'Oh dear,' I said as sympathetically as I could. 'Did it belong to your husband?'

'This is also why I'm leaving!' Margaret jumped to her feet. 'You're just as nosy as Alice Warren was!'

Enquiring after Margaret's husband hardly seemed to be on the same level as a murdering madman loose in the village, but who was I to judge someone else's emotions when my own were far from simple. Still, I thought Margaret's sudden and extreme anger was completely excessive. 'I was simply making conversation. I'm terribly sorry If I've offended you.'

'You village women can't just let things be. You're always poking into things that don't concern you.'

The harshness of her voice made me recall the feeling I experienced when I walked along Margaret's corridor in front of her. It was fear. Only momentary, but fear, nevertheless. Despite the warmth of the day, I shivered. Perhaps it hadn't been such a good idea to shut myself into the parlour with Mrs Leaming. What would I do if she attacked me?

I was being silly. Margaret was leaving the village because of her fear of being killed. She had just told me so. Unless that was all an elaborate ruse and she was really leaving so she didn't get caught. Shaking off my unease, I drew in a deep, calming breath. I was allowing Margaret's histrionics to influence my own thoughts and feelings.

'I am sorry you feel that way,' I mumbled, attempting to look contrite while I hatched what I thought of as a devious plan. 'Alice was extremely friendly and—'

'Alice was a nosy woman who disguised her overzealous curiosity as a part of her role as chairwoman of the committee. She was no better than the rest of the gossipy women in this awful place. I won't be sad to leave. Not one bit.'

I waited until Margaret had finished her tirade before I gave a carefully thought-out response. 'That's why you said you would visit me the day after the show. You didn't want me turning up at your house.'

What was in the house that Margaret didn't want me to know about?

'And yet, that's exactly what you did.'

I got to my feet and cleared my throat. 'There doesn't seem a lot more to say, does there? On behalf of the Westleham Village Committee, I accept your resignation. I wish you well in Cornwall.'

I hoped I sounded a lot more confident than I felt. My knees shook and my throat was dry. I walked to the parlour door and opened it. Margaret got up and flounced past me.

Moments later, the front door slammed closed, and I heaved out a sigh of relief. 'Good day to you, too, Mrs Leaming.'

* * *

As soon as I was sure that Margaret had continued along the lane to her own house, I locked my front door and hurried over the road to the vicarage.

Gertrude Felton, the vicar's housekeeper, answered the door. She looked me up and down. 'Yes?'

Ignoring her bad-mannered tone, I pasted on a bright smile. 'I wondered if I might speak with the vicar.'

'I'm sure the vicar would be better off if he wasn't seen speaking to the likes of you.'

'I don't know what you mean, Mrs Felton.'

'Well then, let me make it perfectly clear to you. I know you told the police about my George. He didn't mean no harm. No one got hurt. All he wanted to do was win a prize for his hard work. He works enough in people's gardens with little thanks. But, oh no, you had to involve yourself and get him arrested. I don't know why you would do that.'

I frowned. Surely the answer to that was obvious. 'George committed a criminal offence. Lots of people had their gardens ruined because of him. I think it's only right that the police investigated his actions. If that led to him being arrested, I can't be held responsible for that. Now, may I please speak to the vicar?'

She glared at me, letting me know in no uncertain terms how much she wished she could slam the door in my face. Eventually, she turned her back and retreated down the corridor before returning moments later.

'The vicar will see you now,' she said grandly.

'Thank you, Mrs Felton. That is very kind of you,' I replied in an equally false solicitous tone. No doubt she had attempted to change her tone now the vicar could hear.

She led me through to Luke's study. It looked very different to the last time I had visited. When Reverend Gibbs was in residence, papers were strewn haphazardly across the top. He frequently lost his glasses in the mess.

Now, things were arranged in neat piles. A small framed photograph sat in one corner. I leaned forward. 'May I?'

'Yes, of course.' He picked up the photo and passed it to me, then turned to Mrs Felton, who was standing in the doorway, staring at us both.

'Tea for two, please, Mrs Felton.'

I walked over to the door after the housekeeper had left.

'Leaving so soon?' he asked with a grin.

'No. Just checking she's gone before I tell you about the extremely strange thing that has just happened.'

'I'm not sure I believe you.'

'What do you mean?'

'What doesn't count as strange in this village? I wager whatever has happened just now isn't nearly as peculiar as the other goings-on in this supposedly quaint little place.'

'You do have a point there.' I looked at the photograph. 'Is this your mother and siblings?'

'Yes, that's right.' He held out his hand, and I walked over and returned the photograph.

'Did your father not like having his photograph taken?' As soon as I spoke, I wished I hadn't said anything, as his face clouded over with an emotion I couldn't name. Margaret Leaming was right – I *was* nosy.

'No,' Luke replied, looking at the photo and back at me. 'He didn't.'

I took the hint and dropped the subject. 'I have just had a visit from Mrs Leaming. She has given me her resignation as secretary of the village committee. She says she is going to sell up and move to a house that she has in Cornwall. How odd is that?'

'Yes, you're right, that is peculiar.'

'She doesn't seem the type of woman that would own a house in Cornwall, although she never seems badly off. That is, she never speaks about being short of money. I don't suppose those are quite the same thing, are they? Everyone knows I have little money, but I've heard no gossip about Mrs Leaming either way.'

'And she said sell up? As though she owns the house in the village?'

I nodded. 'That is definitely what she said.'

Luke tapped his fingers on the table. I recognised that was a habit he employed when he was thinking. 'Who do we know that works in the estate agent?'

'Well, Mr Finnegan owns it.'

'Yes, yes,' Luke said, waving a hand. 'We don't want him. He won't tell us a thing, will he?'

'Oh, I see what you mean. His secretary is his wife. I don't expect she's going to tell us anything either.'

'How long has Mrs Leaming lived there?'

'I would say about a year.'

'And was there a for sale sign outside the house before she moved in?'

'I don't remember seeing one.'

'So who owns it?'

'It was owned by an elderly lady named Phyllis Jones. She died during the war and the house was empty for some time. Then, as I say, about a year ago Mrs Leaming moved in.'

'But who owns it now?'

'I really don't know. The best person for village gossip is Mrs Burnett or Mrs Garrett.'

Luke smiled. 'Who, it so happens, you're going to see today.'

'And it just so happens I have an idea that I think might win Mrs Garrett round.'

'Are you going to share this brilliant plan?'

I tapped the side of my nose. 'Let's see if it works first. Now, I'm hoping that as a vicar, you'll know the answer to this question. How easy is it to find a copy of a person's marriage certificate?'

'Jolly easy, actually,' Luke replied. 'One simply enquires at Somerset House in London. Whose marriage certificate do we need?'

'I should like to know... That is, I think it would be very interesting to know whether indeed Mrs Leaming has ever actually been married. Can you find that out?'

'Yes, of course. I shall telephone one of my chums and ask him to go to Somerset House for that information.'

'Should we tell Detective Inspector Robertson about Mrs Leaming's intention to leave the village?'

'Do you think it's pertinent to the investigation?' he asked. 'Do you believe she is somehow involved?'

'I think it's extremely coincidental that Margaret is desperate the leave the village after two people have been killed.'

'Perhaps she's truly afraid.'

'Or she's running away before she gets caught.'

'But then why would she cry and seem in such distress? What motive does she have?'

'Maybe she's just a talented actress. She accused me of being nosy, and she said Alice was very nosy, too.'

'People here *are* rather inquisitive, Mrs Miller.'

I blinked as his words hit home. 'I suppose you're right, and here I am happily gossiping away about someone else when I know the damage it can do.'

'Tea, Vicar,' Mrs Felton announced as she sailed into the room and put a tray down on a side table. Her dour presence ended our conversation.

Although she did not acknowledge my presence in the room

at all, Mrs Felton shot a filthy look my way, unseen by Luke, as she left.

* * *

After a hurried cup of tea with Luke, I walked along the lane to Mrs Garrett's cottage.

I would have liked to stay at the vicarage and discuss our case – as I was coming to think of it – longer with Luke. But Mrs Felton, I was certain, was lingering in the hallway, trying to listen to every word of our discussion. Or, worse, she had hurried along to the telephone box outside the post office and was making a telephone call to the bishop about my outrageous behaviour.

It was laughable. I had done nothing scandalous in my life. Beyond doubt, I was the most boring person I knew. Still, if calling on the vicar, in broad daylight, was a crime reportable to the bishop, then Mrs Felton could go ahead.

I knocked on Mrs Garrett's front door before I could change my mind, run back down the lane and work in my garden.

Mrs Garrett looked down her nose at me for a long moment before speaking. 'Yes?'

'Might I come in for a moment, Mrs Garrett?' I adopted the most conciliatory tone I had. 'I have a proposal for you.'

'I can't imagine anything you would have to say would interest me.'

'Yes, I understand how you might feel that way. I'm terribly sorry, but we seem to have got off on the wrong foot. Perhaps what I have to say might go some way to mending the bridge between us.'

I pasted a smile on my lips, which was in direct contrast to the way I was feeling. As far as I knew, and Luke had told me, I had done nothing wrong other than be lucky enough to have a husband who came home from war.

That wasn't really something I could help one way or the other. It was good fortune, not anything to do with something I had or hadn't done. I'm certain I prayed no more, or less, than the next woman. Though perhaps that wasn't the complete truth. I probably had prayed a lot less than other women. Not because I didn't want Stan home, but because I knew I didn't love him as desperately as other women loved their husbands.

I averted my eyes from the mole on the side of Mrs Garrett's face as I tried to imagine her being so frantic about her husband's safe return that she prayed fervently every night. It didn't matter how hard I tried, I just couldn't imagine the woman summoning up that kind of passion. Though, of course, I never would have imagined Charles Warren to show such utter devastation at the loss of his wife, either. What did I know? I had never been in love. Not really.

She stared at me, pursed her lips, then raked her gaze from the toes of my gardening boots to the top of my headscarf. 'You can come through to the kitchen. I don't have time for nonsense, Mrs Miller, so please do not waste my time.'

'No, Mrs Garrett, absolutely not.'

I felt as though I was a naughty school child being taken through to the headmistress's office, where I was almost certainly going to receive the cane.

'Sit there.' She pointed at a chair while she herself took a chair at the head of the table in front of a large brown teapot wearing a bright red cosy.

Yes, ma'am.

Whoever did Mrs Garrett think she was – Queen Elizabeth? Though, I realised, as soon as my bottom touched the chair as instructed, it wasn't so much Mrs Garrett believing she was superior to me but the other way around. I was doing as I was told, because I still saw myself as a schoolgirl, or a woman socially inferior to Mrs Garrett.

'I've come to ask if you would think about taking the role of secretary of the Westleham Village Committee.'

'Think about it?' Mrs Garrett barked.

'I can't officially offer it to you until we convene a meeting. Obviously, we will have to take a vote. But you're a respected member of the village, and I think you would be perfect for the role.' I held my breath. I remembered the committee had approached her in the past but had said she was too busy.

'Why are you asking me now? Don't you have a secretary?'

'Yes. Well, no. Not any more. Mrs Leaming resigned this morning, and I thought you would be the perfect replacement.' Mrs Garrett's kitchen was very warm. A trickle of sweat started between my shoulder blades and rolled its way down my spine. It was definitely the heat and not fear that was causing my body to quake.

'You haven't answered my question. Why me?'

'Like I said,' I said haltingly, 'you're well respected... um... a pillar of the community and... erm... perfect for the job.'

'You don't even know me.' She folded her arms under her bosom and stared at me suspiciously. 'How can you know what I would be good at? Has the vicar sent you?'

I lifted my chin. 'I have just come from the vicarage. But, no, he didn't send me. In fact, I didn't tell him why I was coming here.'

'We've never got along. Why would I want to be your secretary?'

'The *committee* secretary,' I corrected and got to my feet. 'I can see I've wasted my time. If you don't want the job, I shall think of another candidate.'

'I didn't say that,' she blurted. 'Sit back down.'

Perversely, I decided to stand. Either she wanted the job, or she didn't. I certainly would not beg. I had kowtowed to her quite enough for one day.

'Mrs Garrett, do you know who owns the cottage currently occupied by Mrs Leaming?'

She got two cups and saucers down from a cupboard and poured tea into one cup, watching me the entire time. 'Is that why you're really here?'

Weak tea flowed from the spout of the teapot. She added milk and sugar, then took a small sip. I presumed she was giving me some sort of test by deliberately only filling one cup. The only problem was I wasn't at all sure how to pass that test.

'Partly,' I said, deciding honesty was the best policy. Mrs Garrett not only reminded me of a schoolteacher in her manner, but she also shared the same innate sense of knowing when someone was being untruthful. 'I had already decided to come and speak to you this morning. After Mrs Leaming handed me her resignation, I immediately thought to ask you to fill her role.'

Tea that resembled dishwater flowed into the other cup. 'Milk and sugar?'

'Yes, please. Two sugars for me.'

She raised her eyebrows at me, put two heaped spoonfuls into the pale amber liquid and pushed the saucer across the table towards me. I didn't take sugar, but I thought the addition might make the drink somewhat more palatable.

'You want to know about Mrs Leaming's cottage?'

'Yes, please.' I sipped my tea. I carefully schooled my face not to show a grimace as she watched me. If only there were a plant nearby I could fling the tea into while she wasn't looking.

'I'm sure a woman as intelligent as you will have worked out, in the same way I have, that Mrs Leaming seems to manage rather nicely on very little.'

I immediately understood what I had not before. Mrs Garrett had lost her husband. Therefore, the only money she had to rely upon was her husband's army pension. At least Ruby and I could pool our resources and I had my garden. It also explained why Mrs Garrett's tea was so very dreadful. She was probably pouring hot water over day-old leaves to eke out her provisions.

When had I become so wrapped up in my own woes that I failed to see the trials other people were going through in the same village? Shame flooded through me. I had never seen myself as a selfish person, yet that is exactly what I had become.

'I had noticed that. Luke and I—' My voice trailed off as Mrs Garrett's lips flattened. 'That is, the vicar and I had a conversation about Mrs Leaming's financial arrangements just last night.'

'Be very careful, Mrs Miller. It is much easier for people to forget a young girl's mistake than that of a married woman.' She set her teacup down on her saucer. 'Now that cottage was owned by Mrs Jones, as you know. She had two sons and one daughter. All things being equal, you imagine she would've left the house to all three children.'

'So either Mrs Leaming bought the house from them, or she pays them a rental sum?'

'I shall have the answer for you later today.' Mrs Garrett got to her feet, and I took that as my cue to leave.

Draining the last of the awful tea, I placed the cup back into the saucer. 'Thank you, Mrs Garrett, that's very kind. May I ask, do you know the Finnegans at the estate agents very well?'

'Oh, they won't tell me a thing. I shan't be asking them. They are sticklers for confidentiality. Their cleaner, on the other hand, is a very good friend.'

I asked no more. It was probably best I didn't know how Mrs

Garrett's friend was going to gather the information I wanted. 'I look forward to talking later. Thank you, Mrs Garrett.'

'I'll see you out,' she said. 'About the other matter. I shall give it serious thought and let you know my decision after I've had time to sleep on it.'

I nodded. It wasn't until I got back over the road and was walking to my cottage that I realised what she meant. I'd completely forgotten about the vacant role of committee secretary.

12

After a morning of working on the garden, I ate a quick lunch, then walked down the lane to the post office. Everyone just referred to it as that, but being situated as it was in a small village, it was so much more. It was also the only place to buy groceries for a start.

Of course, we had a separate bakery, butcher's, and greengrocer's. These days, however, everything we could afford came in packets or tins and those items were found in Mr Harrington's post office-cum-general store.

'Good afternoon, Mrs Miller.' I was greeted by the round, smiling face of the shop assistant, Mrs Rogers. 'What can I get for you today?'

'Just a single second-class stamp, please.' I had no need for stamps, though simply thinking about them made me realise exactly how long it had been since Ruby or I had written to our parents. We really should write them a note, especially given what was going on in the village. A thought occurred to me. 'Have the murders made the national newspapers, do you know?'

'Goodness me, Mrs Miller, where have you been all week?'

Mrs Rogers shook her head and gave me a kind smile. 'The head-lines over the last few days have been about nothing but the two suspicious deaths.'

My parents would likely know what was going on already then. As would Stan. Despite everything, it hurt that he had not tried to check up on me. If he was alive, wherever he was in the country, he would certainly still take *The Times* every day as he always had.

'How is poor Mr Harrington bearing up?'

'Well, I shouldn't really comment,' Mrs Rogers said, lowering her voice in that way people do when they are about to do exactly what they said they shouldn't. 'But he has taken it remarkably well.'

'And the children?' I enquired. 'I heard Mrs Harrington's mother came and took them to stay with her.'

'Indeed.' Mrs Rogers clicked her tongue in dismay. 'The poor little mites still haven't come back. And, let me tell you, it isn't because Mr Harrington is busy in the shop. He hasn't set foot in the place except for opening and closing times.'

'Goodness,' I said, trying desperately to think of something else intelligent to say to keep the conversation going. 'Perhaps he's been too distraught to do much of anything.'

Mrs Rogers sniffed. 'He's spent enough time in the pub. Though, I suppose, that's what men do, isn't it?'

I didn't really know. Stan had never been much for going to the pub. Not even on special occasions. Come to think of it, other than sitting in his favourite chair with his slippers and newspa-per, he hadn't ever done much of anything.

'I suppose so.' I checked no one had come in behind me, even though I would've heard the bell if they had. 'The person I under-stood to be fond of a drink in that family was Mrs Harrington herself.'

'I wouldn't really know about that myself,' Mrs Rogers said, 'but that is a commonly known fact around the village.'

'Didn't Mrs Harrington help out in the shop at all?'

'Oh, goodness me, no.' Mrs Rogers laughed. 'Not one bit. Of course, she had all those children to look after. That's how I came to be employed here.'

'I thought they had a nanny?'

'Oh yes, they did. I was employed. Then Mrs Harrington wanted to go out and about to all her charitable meetings. So Mr Harrington, bless him, got that young girl in to look after the children.'

'He must have been very devoted to Mrs Harrington,' I murmured.

'Most definitely,' Mrs Rogers agreed. 'Anything she wanted, she got. Mr Harrington was very good like that.'

Which was exactly what Mr Warren had said about his own wife. I don't know what I did wrong. Or was it what they did right? I couldn't even get Stan to put the kettle on, let alone make all my wishes come true.

'Where is the nanny now?'

Mrs Rogers wagged a finger in my direction. 'Don't you go thinking like that, Mrs Miller! The young girl immediately went back to her family in Lambcott. Mr Harrington would never have stood for any gossip. It wouldn't have been right for her to stay in the house with Mrs Harrington and the children gone.'

'No, indeed.' Mrs Rogers handed over a stamp. I dug about in my purse for enough coins to pay. 'Thank you.'

I asked nothing further, as Mrs Rogers appeared to be loyal to Mrs Harrington, but I did want to know the name of the nanny. She would be a very good person to speak to. Working in the house would give her all sorts of inside information about the Harringtons that could be very useful in uncovering Elsie's murderer. I was certain Mrs Garrett would know the name of the nanny. It should then be very simple to find her in the nearby village of Lambcott.

After I left the post office, I stood on the path outside, deciding what to do next. Should I go home or to the pub? Luke had suggested I speak to Mr Harrington. I couldn't imagine Mr Harrington being very talkative to me in the pub, especially if it was busy.

Thinking of the pub reminded me I was still waiting for Joe Noble to settle up with me. I didn't want to tell the police about his illegal alcohol sales, but I didn't want him to get away with underpaying me either.

I set off back home, hatching a plan with every step about how to get paid by Joe, how to meet the nanny, and wondering what Mrs Garrett would say when she came back to me with the information about Phyllis Jones's cottage.

Unlatching my gate, I walked through and spotted a parcel on my doorstep. How odd. I couldn't remember the last time I had received a parcel. Perhaps Ruby had ordered something and forgotten to let me know.

I picked it up and noticed my own name and address written in big block lettering. The parcel was wrapped in plain brown paper and tied with string. I pulled on the string and the paper quickly unravelled in my hands. Something fell out onto the step next to my feet.

I jumped back impulsively, but it took a moment for my mind to catch up and register what was lying next to my work boots.

It was a rat.

A very dead rat.

Tears sprang to my eyes as I opened my mouth and screamed as loudly as I could.

* * *

'Mrs Miller?'

'What's happening?'

'Who's screaming?'

The voices all entered my consciousness at the same time as people hurried out of their houses and along to mine. I could see Luke's head above most of the others as he pushed his way through to the front, opened my gate and reached my side in long strides.

'What on earth has happened?'

I pointed down at the floor, my hands shaking so much I didn't trust my voice to work.

'What is it?' Mrs Burnett called.

'Someone has left a dead animal on Mrs Miller's doorstep,' the vicar called to my neighbour. 'Can you go into the kitchen and put the kettle on?'

I put my hand inside my bag, fumbling around for my door key. 'I... I can't find my key.'

'Here,' he said kindly. 'Let me help you.'

I turned around to hand him my bag and stumbled. He caught me, a hand underneath one elbow and another supporting me around my back.

'What is the meaning of this?' A loud voice boomed over the hum of conversation.

Luke dropped my bag onto the floor. 'Oh, golly.'

I followed his gaze. A short man wearing a purple shirt with a clerical collar proclaimed him as the bishop. *Oh golly, indeed.*

'Reverend Walker?'

'Your Excellency,' he replied.

'Is that young woman drunk?' he bellowed.

'No, Your Excellency. Not at all. Mrs Miller has had a terrible shock. I came over here, as did many of her neighbours, upon hearing her scream of distress.'

'Hmph,' the bishop replied, looking at the people crowding in the lane outside my gate. 'Let's take this inside. This is not a conversation to have on the street with the entire parish listening.'

'I couldn't agree more.' Luke eventually found my key and unlocked the front door. He had recovered his earlier control.

'You!' The bishop pointed at Mrs Burnett. 'Who are you?'

Maud bobbed into an untidy curtsy. 'Mrs Maud Burnett. I live next door. I must make tea for Mrs Miller.'

It was all so surreal. Someone had sent me a dead rat. The bishop had turned up in Westleham – something I hadn't heard of ever happening before – and Maud was curtsying as though the clergyman was the king himself.

An irrational bubble of laughter gurgled up and threatened to burst free. I pressed my fingers tightly over my mouth as Maud hurried along the corridor towards the kitchen.

'Has anyone seen PC Bottomley? He must come and secure this evidence immediately. I also think he should call DI Robertson to come over from Slough as soon as he can.' Luke gestured to someone in the crowd.

Relieved that someone else was taking care of things, I shuffled along the corridor and opened the door to the parlour.

Desperate to escape to the sanctuary of my kitchen and indulge in a fortifying cuddle with Lizzie, I turned to the bishop, who hovered in the doorway. 'Please take a seat. I shall put the kettle on.'

'*You* will not. I must speak to you on a matter of great importance. Mrs Burnett seems quite capable of making tea by herself.'

I rather thought a tall glass of straight plum gin was more in order after the week I'd had, but I dare not suggest it. Perhaps after he had left, I could indulge in a little tipple and some time to try to come to terms with everything that had happened.

The bishop took my usual chair near the window. I chose the sofa, which would leave the seat opposite the bishop for Luke. I had no desire to sit opposite such a stern-looking man.

Luke entered the parlour, looked at me, then at the bishop. 'It's an unexpected pleasure to see you in Westleham, Your Excellency.'

'It's unexpected,' he confirmed, 'but there's nothing pleasurable about it.'

Luke closed the door firmly and sat on the remaining chair. Stan's chair. I jammed my hands between my thighs to keep them still, though there was nothing I could do about the obvious tremble in my legs.

The bishop stared at me in disgust, then looked over at Luke. 'Are you sure this woman isn't drunk?'

'No,' he said calmly. 'Mrs Miller has been the victim of a quite terrible practical joke. Someone sent her a parcel containing a dead animal.'

'It was a rat,' I said, my voice sounding overloud in the enclosed room.

'What was a rat?' the bishop asked, enunciating every word.

'The dead animal,' I said, feeling foolish.

'Reverend Walker.' He turned to Luke, obviously deciding I wasn't worth talking to. 'I will get straight to the point.'

'Thank you, Your Excellency. I would appreciate that. I'm certain the village constable will wish to interview Mrs Miller.'

'Why would that have anything to do with you?'

'Mrs Miller, as a valued member of this parish, may need my support,' Luke said. 'And quite possibly my spiritual guidance after such a traumatic event.'

'It is my understanding that you and *your parishioner* have enjoyed a particularly close relationship since your arrival in the village.'

My cheeks flushed, which was incredibly annoying. Other than a few indulgent daydreams, I had done nothing of which I should be ashamed.

'I'm afraid I don't know what you are referring to,' Luke said in a voice so calm it was getting on my nerves. How could he be relaxed when someone had attacked his reputation?

'Do you deny several *clandestine* meetings with Mrs Miller?'

'I most certainly do.' Luke leaned forward slightly, but his relaxed tone did not alter. 'In the strongest of terms.'

The bishop pulled a letter from his inside breast pocket. 'I have received a letter from someone who calls themselves "a concerned Westleham resident". They say that your relationship has crossed the boundaries of propriety.'

I reached out a hand. 'May I see the letter?'

'I don't see what difference seeing the letter will do, Mrs Miller. Either you're guilty, or you're not.'

'The vicar has been to dinner on one occasion,' I said, my voice a flat monotone. 'My sister was present. We have walked my dog together, out in the open. We talked about the vicar's experiences in the war and my missing husband. I visited the vicarage this morning in the housekeeper's presence. I can assure you there is nothing improper about our relationship.'

'Why do you think someone sent you a dead rat?'

His sudden change of direction caught me off guard. I blinked. 'I can only think it has something to do with the murders.'

'Why would you be a target of such viciousness?' The bishop sounded almost sympathetic.

I allowed myself to relax slightly. 'It must be because I am trying to find out who the murderer is. Perhaps they are trying to scare me.'

'There was a note,' Luke said reluctantly.

'In the parcel?'

'Yes.' He looked at me as he spoke. 'I'm sorry.'

Icy fingers danced across my skin, leaving goosebumps in their wake. 'What did the note say?'

'It said if you didn't stop investigating, you would end up as dead as the rat. Or words to that effect.'

I nodded slowly. 'I thought that was the implied threat.'

'That is not implied, Mrs Miller,' the bishop said. 'It's explicit. I presume the police are on their way?'

'I have sent someone to find the village policeman,' Luke confirmed.

'Do you have something to do with this *investigation*?' The bishop raised an eyebrow at Luke.

'As the vicar of this parish, I do feel it is within my remit to ensure safety for the village.'

The bishop fluttered the letter in the air. 'It is your *remit* to care for the spiritual welfare of the parish, not to involve yourself in police business. You are endangering yourself and, more importantly, this woman with your endeavours.'

'I'm quite capable of imperilling myself.' I got to my feet and walked over to the bishop, glad my legs supported my weight even though they wobbled more than those of a newborn foal. 'Please, may I see the letter?'

Wordlessly, he passed it over to me and I studied it. The words were not important to me. I was looking at the handwriting.

'Do you see anything important, Mrs Miller?' Luke asked.

'The writing is Mrs Harrington's.'

'Isn't she that unfortunate woman who died in her bed?'

I sighed. 'Yes, that's correct. She must have sent the letter before she died.'

The letter's insinuations gave me an exceptionally good reason to want to quiet Mrs Harrington once and for all. I looked at Luke helplessly. This mystery was like a ball of wool after a cat had played with it: the threads were hopelessly tangled and no matter how hard you tried to unravel it, you just ended up in a worse mess.

'That's very unfortunate.' The bishop held out a hand and I returned the letter to him.

I wanted to laugh. It was worse than unlucky. It was downright tragic. I was being targeted even from beyond the grave.

'I think we—'

'No.' The bishop held up a hand and stared at Luke, the earlier sympathy now gone from his voice. 'It seems it's a bit too late for you to start thinking, Reverend Walker. Go back to the vicarage and stay away from both the investigation and Mrs Miller. Otherwise, I *will* have to consider sanctions.'

'For carrying out my duties?' Luke asked boldly.

'For interfering in other people's duties. You are here on my good grace alone. I can remove that at any time, and you would do well to remember that.' He pointed to the door. 'Now, go. And see where that infernal woman is with the tea. Has she gone all the way to India for it?'

After Luke left, the bishop turned back to me. 'Is it correct that you are a married woman?'

'Yes,' I replied. 'My husband left for work just over a year ago and has never returned. The police can find no trace of him.'

'Are you a suspect in his disappearance?'

'I am not.' I looked out of the window at the crowd of neighbours still gathered around my gate. 'At least not in the eyes of the police. As for my neighbours in the village, their thoughts on the subject are somewhat more fanciful.'

'You believe this letter to be malicious?'

'I most certainly do.' I nodded. 'Though I can see that, from your point of view, you may believe there is no smoke without fire.'

'My duty is not to assess the veracity of the gossip of this village,' he said. 'It is to ensure the spiritual welfare of *everyone* is being served. You do see that, don't you?'

'Yes.'

'Can I trust you will help the new vicar to attend to all of his flock equally?'

'Of course,' I said flatly. 'I will discourage the vicar from spending any time with me that will not help him carry out his parish duties.'

'Thank you, Mrs Miller. I shall see myself out.'

As he opened the parlour door, Mrs Burnett sailed in, her paisley-patterned housedress billowing against her robust calves. 'Here we are.'

'Where on earth have you been?' the bishop asked.

'Call of nature, Your Excellency.'

I smothered a laugh that I feared was more hysterical than amusement.

He shook his head. 'I must get on with my duties. Good day, ladies.'

As soon as the front door closed, Maud flopped onto the sofa next to me. 'Now, don't you worry, dear. I heard every single word. For now, I will be your go-between. Everything you need to tell the vicar can go through me, and vice versa. You can't give up now.'

She patted my hand, and to my horror, I promptly burst into tears.

* * *

Some hours later, after speaking to PC Bottomley and regaling Ruby with the events of the day, I sat alone in the parlour. Well, without another human, that was. I remembered this time last week I was bemoaning the fact I had no one to talk to. Whilst today, I hadn't been alone since the moment I awoke. Being sociable was quite exhausting. Yet I wasn't ready to sleep.

'I'll miss seeing the vicar as often,' I told Lizzie. 'He's such a comfort.'

Dogs can't raise their eyebrows in disbelief, but everything about Lizzie's expression was doubtful.

'All right, I'll miss his pretty blue eyes and his capable manner.'

She thumped her tail on the floor.

'I wish there was something I could do.' I looked down at my knitting, but I wasn't in the mood to make more mistakes in a pattern that was beyond my skill level and didn't even have an intended recipient.

The wireless was silent. I turned that off when Ruby went to bed. Usually, I found its sound comforting, but this evening, I was too on edge to have the added noise when there was enough in my own head.

'I know. I'll go through Alice's notes. Maybe there will be something in there that explains why Margaret Leaming has decided to leave Westleham so suddenly.'

I opened the small bureau in the corner of the room that Stan had used to keep bills and his cheque book. Finding a pen and some paper, I went through to the kitchen.

I'd hidden the box containing Alice's notes in the pantry behind a sack of potatoes. Retrieving them, I placed them on the kitchen table and pulled the piece of paper towards me.

I divided the page into four columns, then gave each of them a header:

Name
Motive
Means
Opportunity.

Under the first column, I wrote: *Joe Noble, George Felton, Charles Warren, Ada Garrett, Margaret Leaming.* Turning the page over, I replicated the process – one side for Alice, the other for Elsie.

I didn't really believe Mrs Garrett was guilty of anything other than being a lonely woman who liked to gossip too much, but four suspects seemed too few.

'If I've got Charles down, it seems only fair I add Ernest.' I looked at Lizzie. 'What do you think?'

She opened one eye and wagged her tail. I took that to be a yes, which pleased me. Six suspects looked so much neater on the page than five.

I filled in each section of my suspect analysis, as I called it, then returned to the bureau for an envelope. I would ask Maud to deliver the note to the vicar in the morning. He could then add his thoughts to the document. Perhaps seeing everything written out would make things clearer to one of us.

I then started going through the box of village committee files, one section at a time. It was a long shot, but maybe there was something in her notes that would give me a clue as to why she was murdered.

When I thought I simply couldn't go on as Margaret Leaming's handwriting was so terrible, and Alice's wasn't much better, I saw something that made no sense.

The document seemed to be a plan about who was to man what stalls at the show. Innocuous enough. It was a typewritten sheet with the location of the table, what they would show on it and who was in charge. Most of the information was already typed, but Alice had handwritten the individuals' names.

I couldn't remember being at the meeting for this, which made no sense – I had been involved in every step of the planning. But then the date finally made sense; that was the day I'd taken Lizzie to the vet for her annual check-up. Alice and Margaret had met at Margaret's house in case they needed to use the typewriter.

Which was all very tedious. Except for something Alice had written in the top left-hand corner. It had nothing to do with the show, and I couldn't think of any reason for Alice to write it.

She had written: *Sheraton?*

The only time I had heard that word recently was when Margaret Leaming had said the sideboard I admired in her home was not genuine. I couldn't imagine why Alice would have written the furniture maker on a document setting out the plan for the village show.

13

The following day, I was still puzzling over the peculiar notation I'd found. It made even less sense to me this morning than it had yesterday.

Ruby was reluctant to go to work and leave me after learning what had happened. She made me promise to stay home, unless it was a dire emergency, and keep all the doors locked. I hoped she considered visiting the Harringtons' nanny as necessary because I intended to go there as soon as I found out where she lived.

The door knocker sounded as I was about to go into the garden. I went into the parlour and peeked through the net curtains to see who was at the door. Ruby would be so proud of me.

I hurried to the door. 'Detective Inspector.'

'Good morning, Mrs Miller.'

'Come in,' I said. 'Do you have news?'

'I do.' He hung his hat on the stand and followed me through to the parlour. 'Please don't trouble yourself to put on the kettle, this will only be a short visit.'

'Have you found out who sent the parcel?'

He glanced at the doorway. 'We have found out that it was left on your doorstep, as opposed to being sent through the postal system.'

I drew in a breath. 'I could have told you that. The parcel didn't have any type of stamp on it, so it was rather obvious it was hand delivered. And if you're looking for my sister, she's at work.'

'I wasn't—' His ears turned pink. 'Because the parcel was hand delivered, it will be very difficult to trace who sent it. Everything is generic. From the paper used to wrap it, to the string, and the writing was in block capitals.'

'None of that is news.'

'The information I have come to share with you concerns the murders. Regarding the package, I wanted to let you know we are looking into it. To put your mind at rest.'

'I'm afraid you can't do that.' A shudder rippled through my body as I remembered my horror when the dead animal fell out of the wrapping paper. 'Two of my neighbours have been murdered, and now it seems I am being targeted. Tell me how you are going to make me feel safe?'

'Two uniformed police officers are to patrol the village,' he said. 'That should deter the fiend.'

'Cyril Bottomley *lives* here and has provided no deterrent whatsoever,' I snapped. 'The only way I will feel safe in my own home again is when I have uncovered the murderer.'

'I understand your frustration.' He pushed a thick piece of blonde wavy hair back from his forehead. 'However, you must leave the investigations to me. Not only is it my job, but I have the experience and expertise that you do not. Not to mention attempting to uncover the murderer yourself could place you in unnecessary danger.'

'What's the news?' I didn't want to argue with him, I just

wanted him to tell me the latest and leave the house so my neighbours could visit and start filling me in on the information they had discovered.

'The pathologist is quite certain both ladies were killed with cyanide. I hope to narrow down the suspects quickly by searching everyone's home and garden.'

I barked out a short laugh. 'Well, that's a pointless exercise, Inspector. Let me tell you that now. There will be many people in Westleham who keep a quantity of cyanide in their garden shed.'

'Why would anyone keep a deadly poison in their shed?'

I smiled. 'You do not live in the country, so I can excuse your ignorance. Cyanide is routinely used for destroying wasp nests. It is also found in rat poison.'

He raised an eyebrow at that information. 'Who is likely to have the stuff?'

'I have it,' I admitted. 'Anyone else who is a serious gardener will have it. George Felton will almost certainly have some. Are you aware he is the Harringtons' gardener?'

'Yes, I am.' The detective bristled. 'As I've already said, we are happy with the alibi he has given for both murders.'

'I have some information to share with you,' I told him. 'It might mean nothing. Or it might mean something very important indeed. Last night I went through Alice's papers. They are mostly committee documentation, so not at all interesting. However, she had made a handwritten note on the side of one page. It has no relevance to the subject matter, which is all typewritten.'

'What did she write?'

'Just one word,' I said, feeling foolish. '"Sheraton".'

'Sheraton?' He frowned. 'As in the furniture?'

'It struck me as odd, because when I was in Mrs Leaming's home on Sunday afternoon, I commented on the striking sideboard in her parlour. She was very quick to assure me it is a fake.

I brushed it off as there was something very peculiar about her whole demeanour that day.'

'I can't investigate someone based on strange behaviour, I'm afraid. I need evidence.'

'Then you shall have to pay her a visit and get the evidence you need quickly,' I told him. 'She told me she is selling up and leaving the village. That's odd too, isn't it?'

'Did she tell you why she is leaving?'

I spread my hands out, palms up. 'She *told* me it was because she was afraid.'

'You don't believe that?'

'I don't.' I wished there was some way of making him see what was as plain as the nose on his face – Margaret Leaming was hiding something. 'You must speak to her.'

'All right,' he agreed. 'I will visit her while I am in the village, though I'm not sure it will do any good. What motive does she have?'

'I don't know,' I admitted. 'She was quite ferocious when she came to see me yesterday morning. Accused both Alice and me of being nosy.'

The detective squirmed in his seat, and I could tell he thought the same as the vicar – people in Westleham could be overly inquisitive. 'Again, I can't really investigate someone based on—'

'Just go and see her,' I said crossly. 'All I am trying to do is help you by pointing you in the right direction. While you're there, you might find out who does her garden, and how she pays for the service.'

'What connection does that have?'

I didn't want to say 'I don't know' again despite the truth of the words. If I knew what it all meant, there would be no need for him. The murderer would already be unmasked and Westleham could get back to normal instead of me suspecting my neighbours

– and, in turn, being suspected myself. Other than Maud, of course. I was quite certain that if that lady wanted me dead, I'd already be laid in the graveyard.

'She always has money,' I told him. 'Apparently, she owns a house in Cornwall. But none of it has the ring of truth. She appeared in the village suddenly and no one really knows anything about her, but the more I find out, the less it makes sense.'

'Is there anyone in the village you do trust, Mrs Miller?'

'Myself, Ruby, and perhaps the vicar.'

'That's it?' He smiled. 'And the vicar only rates a "perhaps"?'

I shrugged. 'He *appears* trustworthy, but I haven't known him long enough to be certain. There are many secrets in a small village, Inspector. Most people have at least one. Perhaps someone has killed to keep theirs from becoming public knowledge.'

He got to his feet. 'I should get on. Please remember what I said, Mrs Miller. There will be uniformed police in the village. I do hope that helps to make you feel safer.'

It was clear that he thought I was talking nonsense and humouring me rather than taking my concerns seriously. If only I was more eloquent and could explain what I meant better instead of sounding like a paranoid fool.

'My sister usually gets home from work around six if you would like to come back and update me on your progress around then?'

'That shouldn't be necessary,' he said stiffly.

'Oh, what a shame.' I smiled wickedly. 'She will be sorry to have missed you.'

'Will she?' he asked quickly. Too quickly for a man pretending he wasn't interested.

'Maybe you could pop by and reassure her?' I suggested. 'I'm sure she would be most grateful.'

'Yes... Um... I will see if I have time.' He marched into the hallway and grabbed his hat from the stand. 'Until later, Mrs Miller.'

I let him out as Maud Burnett hurried up the path with the envelope I gave her earlier this morning to take over to the vicar.

'Good day, Inspector.'

* * *

'This is very exciting!' Maud said as she hurried inside, her cheeks flushed. 'I feel just like a spy!'

We went through to the kitchen. She opened the envelope and pulled out the single sheet I'd written my deductions on the previous evening. In red ink, Luke had written: *There is no obvious connection between these two murders.* The statement wasn't at all useful. I knew that. It was the reason I had put my thoughts down on paper.

'The vicar hasn't come up with anything new.' I couldn't hide the disappointment in my voice.

'On the contrary,' Maud said. 'There's more.'

With a lack of patience, she took out a smaller piece of paper. 'What's that?'

'The information you asked Luke to get on Mrs Leaming.' Maud's eyes danced. 'She's never been married. At least, not under the name of Margaret Leaming.'

'I'm not sure I understand.'

'The vicar's friend said no one named Margaret Leaming in the right age range has ever married. Either as Margaret Leaming, or to become Margaret Leaming upon marriage. I don't know about you, but I think lying about a dead husband is very poor form.'

'I agree completely.' I tapped a pen against the paper. 'It means she's both a liar and a thoroughly unpleasant person, but that doesn't make her a murderer.'

'The vicar thinks it explains why she was so nice to you after Mrs Warren's death.'

'How so?'

'He said she was pleasant to you so she could find out what you knew.'

'And no doubt she hoped being nice meant I wouldn't consider her a suspect. Silly woman. I suspect everyone.'

'Even me?' Maud asked gleefully. 'How exciting!'

'I've decided it couldn't possibly be you or the vicar.'

'Oh, I shouldn't write the vicar off. I'm certain he's capable of deep feelings.'

'He has only been in the village for a few days,' I protested. 'Not nearly enough time to hate someone enough to kill them.'

'I suppose that's true,' Maud said. 'Does that mean Ada Garrett is still on your list? She will be devastated. I think she quite likes you now.'

'Really?' I looked down at the boxes on the paper. The ones next to her name were mostly empty. I couldn't think of a motive for her to kill either woman, or an opportunity for her to get near enough to Mrs Harrington to poison her.

'She didn't mention Stan once,' Maud reported.

'Well, that's definite progress,' I agreed. 'Was she able to find anything out about who owns the cottage Mrs Leaming is living in?'

'Yes, indeed.' Maud pulled a folded piece of paper from a side pocket in her handbag. 'The cottage is owned by Mrs Jones's children through a trust. The trust rents the house to Mrs Leaming.'

She looked up from the page to ensure I was still listening. 'Go on.'

'This is the interesting bit,' she said, as though I hadn't already worked that out. 'The deposit was paid by cheque. The name on the cheque *is not* Mrs Leaming. That person also sends payment directly to the estate agents on the first of every month.'

'Who pays the rent?'

'Arthur Wade.'

My excitement waned. I wasn't sure what name I was expecting to hear, but I hadn't heard of this man. Yet another puzzle piece that made no sense.

'How did Mrs Garrett find out that information?'

'I only know what she told the vicar, which was that the cleaner at the estate agent located the information.'

'Located? What does that mean?'

Maud lifted a shoulder. 'I know no more than I've already told you.'

We knew more information, but it gave us no greater degree of clarity. 'Did Mrs Garrett know the name of the Harringtons' nanny?'

'Yes, she is called Nancy Turner, and she lives in Lambcott, three doors down from the church.'

'I shall have to catch the bus.' I got up and rummaged through a drawer. 'There's a timetable in here somewhere, I'm sure.'

'Do you really think that's a good idea?'

'How else am I going to talk to Nancy if I don't go see her?' I found the leaflet I was looking for and sat back down.

'I would hate for something to happen to you,' Maud said, a concerned look making the wrinkles on her face stand out even more than usual. 'You're a very quiet neighbour. Imagine if we had the same trouble here as they had in Winteringham!'

Everyone knew about the problems caused in Winteringham,

a nearby village, when a parent with too much money and not enough sense allowed his son use of his cottage in the centre of the village. The boy's parents lived in London and never visited the house that had once belonged to an elderly aunt. It was a very foolhardy arrangement. I didn't have children, but even I knew the things unsupervised young men could get up to – none of them were good.

'Thank you, Mrs Burnett,' I said. 'I shall feel better knowing you are worried about my safety.'

Neither of us had mentioned me breaking down in tears the previous evening. I'm not sure which of us was most embarrassed by the outpouring of emotion.

'Now, the vicar also said I must remember to mention that Florence Noble *did not* make the drinks she put onto her tray and served. She said when she went into the marquee, they were on the table already poured. She thought you had done it.'

'That wasn't me.' I frowned. 'I put the glasses on the table upside down so they would be ready for Florence to fill.'

'Oh dear,' Mrs Burnett said. 'I don't think the vicar has filled that in on your form. Should he have?'

Never mind my scrappy piece of paper. This information was more important than how I had organised my scattered thoughts.

'I'll be right back.' I went into the parlour and extracted another couple of sheets of paper from the bureau. It was thick and of good quality, the type that one uses to write letters to people when wanting to make a statement. Not the sort that I should use to write down my thoughts about a murderer.

I paused in the doorway and looked back at the bureau. How many times had I seen Stan sitting there of an evening writing letters? Too many to count. I couldn't remember if I had ever asked him to whom he was corresponding. If I had, I no longer recalled the answer.

It felt rather irreverent to use Stan's special writing paper for my detecting efforts. A little thrill of excitement skittered through me. I quite liked the idea that Stan would be displeased at both my using his paper and my efforts to find a murderer. But Stan wasn't here any more, and doing as he wanted during our marriage hadn't done me any good, so I would jolly well start doing more as I pleased now that he wasn't around to chastise me.

'What else do you need to write?' Maud asked as I sat back at the kitchen table.

'Other things,' I said. I held up a hand as she opened her mouth to speak again. 'That is to say, on this page we have names, means, motive, and opportunity. On this page, I shall write things we know but that make no sense. I will use the other piece of paper to write a list of things we still need to find out.'

'You are clever, Mrs Miller,' Maud said. 'Whoever would've guessed?'

I smiled, deciding to take notice only of the first part of Maud's sentence. 'Now, let's get on with our task. The bus leaves in forty-five minutes and I must be on it if I want to talk to Nancy and get back in time to make supper for Ruby.'

* * *

A fortifying cup of tea and jam sandwich later, I was on the bus on the way to Lambcott. The only respite from the stifling heat in the rickety old vehicle was when the door opened and closed to let passengers on and off.

Instead of my usual clothes of old blouse and gardening trousers, I wore a dress fished from the far left-hand side of my wardrobe. On the right side of the wardrobe, Stan's shirts, trousers, pullovers, and his one good suit still hung neatly as though waiting for their owners to come back and wear them. The other side was for my clothes. Shoved against the side were the few dresses I'd worn for work. I hadn't touched those garments in over six years. Not since the day I stopped working – which was the day before I married Stan.

The dress was now an extremely faded grey, but a lot more appropriate for visiting than my usual gardening attire or the serviceable everyday dresses I usually wore – those had been hand-me-downs from my mother and had seen much better days.

As the bus drew to a stop in the centre of Lambcott, I counted the third house along from the church. It was a pretty little cottage with bottle-green ivy climbing up the side. I could see rose bushes in the front garden and, instinctively, knew I was going to like these people. How could I fail to, given they kept an immaculate garden?

I knocked on the door, hoping they would invite me inside and that they had cool refreshments in their refrigerator. Although my dress was smart, it wasn't made for the summer. I longed for one of those floaty creations that swirled around the mid-calf of the models who wore them in the magazines Ruby brought home. Though that was silly. I had no need for pretty dresses when I spent most of my time on my knees in the garden, tending vegetables.

'Yes?' A middle-aged woman peered at me through thick spectacles. 'How can I help you?'

'Is this the correct house for Nancy Turner?'

'It is.' The woman folded her arms. 'I am her mother. Who are you?'

'I'm Martha Miller, from Westleham.' I put out a hand in greeting. 'Pleased to meet you.'

'Likewise, I'm sure.' Mrs Turner looked at me suspiciously. 'What can we do for you?'

'I wondered if I might have a word with Nancy, please? It's very important.'

'About what?' She wasn't hostile, but there was no friendliness in the other woman's tone.

'Mum, who is it?' A youthful voice sounded behind Mrs Turner.

'Never you mind,' her mother replied. 'Go back into the kitchen.'

'Please, Mrs Turner,' I said. 'I really must speak with Nancy.'

'With me?' the girl asked, coming to stand directly behind her mother.

Of course, I had seen Nancy around the village with the Harrington children, but I had never seen her close up before now. She was exceptionally beautiful. Big blue-green eyes dominated her face, which was framed by thick, dark hair. I thought she looked just like magazine pictures of Vivien Leigh.

'Yes, if you have time, I would appreciate it. I shan't take up much of your time.'

'You're from Westleham, aren't you?' Nancy scrutinised me over her mother's shoulder.

'That's right.'

'It can't hurt,' the girl said to her mother. 'You can stay in the room the whole time if you're worried.'

'Of course I am worried,' Mrs Turner retorted. 'You worked for a woman in that village who is now *dead*.'

Somehow Mrs Turner managed to make it sound as though it was Mrs Harrington's own fault she had died. Or maybe she believed there was some sort of shame attached to Nancy because she had lived in a house where a woman had been killed.

'Let's go through to the parlour, Mother.' Nancy pushed the door wider. 'Come along, Mrs Miller.'

Despite Mrs Turner's bluster, it was clear that the person in control of the situation was Nancy.

Nancy took a seat in an extremely comfortable-looking armchair next to the fireplace. Her mother stationed herself directly behind her daughter. I sat opposite and returned Nancy's friendly smile. 'Thank you for agreeing to speak with me.'

'I miss the children,' she said. 'Do you happen to know how they are?'

'I'm afraid not.' I set my handbag on the floor next to my feet. 'They haven't returned to the village. I believe Mrs Harrington's mother came and took them to live with her for the meantime.'

'Probably because their father is disgracefully lecherous and their mother was quite mad.' Mrs Turner drew her lips into such a thin line, they almost disappeared.

'Now, Mother,' Nancy said patiently. 'That's not entirely accurate.'

'Would you mind telling me the truth of it?' I asked.

'I might not mind if you would tell me why you would like to know. I may not work for the Harringtons any more, but I do believe in loyalty towards the people who employed me.'

'That's very admirable.' I liked Nancy very much. She seemed an honest girl, not flighty and silly like so many her age. 'I'm here because I am trying to solve the murders. Now, I know that might sound rather a far-fetched ambition, but I think I can find out more from people in the village than the police, and I should very much like things to go back to normal.'

Nancy nodded once, signifying she had decided to speak to me. 'Mr Harrington is an important man in Westleham, but he's not a very nice man. He was quite rude to poor Mrs Harrington, though she did drink rather much more than was good for her.'

'Do you think she drank *because* he was unkind, or was it more the other way around?'

She thought for a moment. 'I hadn't considered that before now, but I think you're right. Mrs Harrington always seemed to drink more after they had exchanged unpleasant words.'

'That's not quite the same,' I said. 'Exchanging them means Mrs Harrington was also being unkind.'

'It's like this, Mrs Miller.' Nancy flushed slightly and lowered her gaze to her lap. 'Mr Harrington would come home and pick fault with something Mrs Harrington had done or not done. He was always very nice to me, by the way. Then Mrs Harrington would cry and shout back that if he was so displeased by her, he should divorce her and marry his "fancy lady".'

'Goodness me,' I said. 'What a terrible state of affairs.'

'You can see why I wouldn't want my daughter in a household like that,' Mrs Turner said. 'Excessive use of alcohol and a man with a wandering eye. My Nancy is a good girl, but living with those two it wouldn't be long before her reputation was ruined.'

'Quite. Yes, I can see how that could easily happen.' Nancy was such an attractive girl, it wouldn't have taken long before people heard Mrs Harrington's accusations and attached the blame to Nancy. 'Did you ever see any evidence of Mr Harrington's philandering?'

'No, I did not, and he never behaved improperly towards me.' Nancy bit her lip. 'That is, he never approached me, but there were times I didn't like the way he looked at me.'

'I'm very sorry that happened to you.' I recalled Mrs Rogers at the post office telling me that Ernest Harrington had spent a good deal of time at the pub. It occurred to me now that I wasn't sure if that was something he had regularly done, or if it was only since Elsie's death. 'Did Mr Harrington go out after they argued?'

'Always.' Nancy nodded her head emphatically. 'Mrs Harrington never confided in me, but I would imagine she was as sure as I was that when Mr Harrington left the house, it was to see his *mistress*.'

Nancy's voice lowered further, as though she were uttering a swear word. Mrs Turner tutted. 'Disgraceful.'

'Do you know who it was?'

'No, it wasn't my business. I did my best to shield the children from what was going on. That was my job.'

'Did Mr Harrington spend a lot of time at the pub?'

'He went out a lot of an evening,' Nancy said carefully. 'I couldn't say where he went.'

'Were there any signs of an affair that you noticed?' I recalled the things Stan had done that meant nothing at the time, but afterwards added up to him having a secret he did his utmost to keep from me. 'Writing letters and then hiding them if someone came into the room, going out to use the telephone at odd times, not coming home from work at the usual hour. That sort of thing.'

Nancy opened her mouth to answer, then closed it again. I held my breath while she thought through my question. 'I was going to say no, but I suppose those are all things a wife would notice, not me. The children kept me very busy, so I wasn't always aware of what Mr Harrington was doing. There was something that happened occasionally that was odd, though. I did think it strange at the time, but I wanted to keep my job, so I didn't question it.'

'What was it?' I asked eagerly, leaning forward as though that would make Nancy's answer come more quickly.

'Every now and again, when I had my afternoon off, Mr Harrington would ask me to post a letter for him. That wouldn't be a strange thing for any employer to ask, but, of course, the Harringtons owned the post office. Why didn't he just take the letter to work with him and post it himself.'

'A very good question. Did you come to any conclusions?'

'Only that Mr Harrington can't have wanted anyone to see him posting the letter.'

'I don't suppose you happened to notice the address on the letter?'

'It was addressed to a man in Edgecumbe, but I'm afraid I don't remember the name or the address.'

'Thank you, Nancy, you have been very helpful.'

'Now, Mrs Miller,' Mrs Turner said. 'You are to stay right where you are. I will go into the kitchen and bring a tray of cold drinks. You must have worked up a thirst on the bus over and after all that talking.'

'That's very kind,' I replied. 'I should like that very much.'

'It's another fifty minutes until the bus comes,' Nancy said. 'You might as well make yourself comfortable until then. Now Mum knows she doesn't need to worry about you, she'll come back with a tray laden with all sorts of lovely things. You just see if she doesn't.'

Nancy was right. Her mother did return with cold drinks, sandwiches and even some fruit scones. I allowed myself to relax and chat with the Turner women until it was time to leave for home.

All too soon, it was time to catch the bus and return to real life. As the bus trundled through the countryside, I considered what I had learned from Nancy and what it meant for the investigation.

Who had Ernest Harrington been writing to in Edgecumbe and did that have something to do with the affair Nancy was sure he was involved in?

14

As I walked down the lane towards my house, Maud hurried down her path to stall my progress. 'Cooee, Mrs Miller!'

'Good afternoon, Mrs Burnett.'

'The vicar is in my house,' she whispered.

'Then why are you out here?'

'To let you know.' Maud looked left and right, then back at me. She was taking her role far too seriously. Rather than look like a spy, she simply appeared furtive. If anyone was watching her, they would think her behaviour highly suspicious. 'You are to go into your garden, through the gate at the end, and into my garden. I have unlatched my gate, so all you need do is simply push it open. The vicar says he has something enormously important to tell you.'

'What is it?'

'He said I'm not to tell you.' Maud made an impatient movement with her hand. 'Hurry along, Mrs Miller, I am eager for you to hear what he has to say.'

I unlocked my door and went into the house, absently patting Lizzie on the head as I hurried to the back door. Although I longed to take off my shoes and shove my hot feet into the rain barrel at the bottom of the garden, that would have to wait. They needed me next door.

Leaving Lizzie in my garden, I slipped through my gate and into Mrs Burnett's garden. She was already waiting for me at her back door. 'Hurry!'

No sooner had I stepped inside than Mrs Burnett pulled the door closed behind us and turned the key. 'You never lock your doors.'

'You *should* lock yours,' she retorted. 'Don't you know there is a murderer *rampaging* around the village?'

I wanted to laugh at her choice of words, but my eyes fell on the vicar sitting at Maud's kitchen table. Goodness, it seemed like forever since I had last seen him, though, in reality, it was only the previous afternoon.

'I'm glad to see you're home safe, Mrs Miller.'

'Thank you, Vicar,' I said awkwardly. 'You're looking very cool.'

He wore a white shirt, as usual, but he had the cuffs rolled up, showing off powerful forearms. I'd never thought of a vicar having muscles before – they certainly didn't get them from writing sermons or christening babies.

'Does that pass as flirting these days?'

'Mrs Burnett!' I choked. 'I simply meant the vicar looks the opposite of hot. Not cool—'

'Oh, do hush, Mrs Miller.' Maud shook her head as though I had deeply disappointed her. 'We shall talk about this later.'

Never mind putting my feet in the rain barrel to reduce my temperature. If I put my head in there right now, steam would rise. I was so embarrassed. There was only one way to cure my ineptness.

'Let's talk about murder,' I said.

'While you have been away, I've been busy.' Luke rested an elbow on the table.

'What have you found out?'

'I can't really take any credit for this,' he said. 'It is all Mrs Garrett and her amazing knowledge. I don't think there's anything that woman doesn't know.'

She certainly knew everyone's business.

'What has she told you?'

'All about Arthur Wade.'

'Arthur Wade?' I repeated. 'The man who pays Margaret Leaming's rent?'

'That's him.'

'How did you come to discuss Arthur Wade with Mrs Garrett?'

Maud took the lid off her teapot, added a few more tea leaves, topped it off with hot water and gave it a good stir. 'Let's all have a nice cup of tea while we're talking.'

I had drunk more tea in the last week than I had the rest of the year altogether. It was the one perk of investigating. Apart from Mrs Garrett's tea, of course. I should be a bit more charitable given she was a poor widow, but personally, I'd rather have no tea than awful tea.

'I simply visited her and asked her if she recognised his name.'

'And she did?'

'Yes, she did,' he confirmed.

'And this is the thrilling part!' Maud poured tea into three cups, her entire body positively wobbling with barely contained excitement at the information.

'How did she know his name?'

'From the newspaper!'

Luke looked at Maud. 'Who's telling this story?'

'Sorry, Vicar.' Maud grinned, looking anything but contrite.

'Why was Arthur Wade in the newspaper?'

'He went to prison,' Luke said quickly, no doubt wanting to get the words out before Maud could interrupt again. 'For selling stolen furniture.'

'Sheraton!'

'Detective Inspector Robertson has gone back to Slough to discuss the case with an antique valuer.'

'Was Mrs Leaming involved in the thefts?'

'The newspaper article that Mrs Garrett remembered mentioned a man who went to prison for stealing furniture from bombed houses. That was why she particularly remembered his name and the case – what sort of person steals from people who have had their homes destroyed? The detective telephoned to Slough and confirmed that this fellow has now been released.'

'So soon?' I took a sip of tea. 'How disgraceful.'

'They could only charge him with one crime.' Luke pulled a disgusted face. 'But the police always thought there were more.'

'Her house is stuffed full of furniture.' I paused, giving myself a moment to think. 'Perhaps that's why her house is so unsanitary. Few people would want to go inside given the awful stench caused by her cats.'

'I think that's why she was in such a state when you visited her on Sunday,' Luke said. 'Mrs Warren had been inside Mrs Leaming's house and realised it was full of antique furniture. Margaret then had to kill Alice to stop her from reporting her to the authorities.'

'You think she panicked when it caused such a commotion?'

'Yes. It backfired on her because then the police were in the village, poking around and asking questions.'

'I don't think it's her,' Maud said.

'Why not? It's plausible.'

'I think it's Charles.'

'Is that because you heard the rumour that he has a female friend?'

'Yes. So he killed Alice so he can claim the insurance money and be with his new lady.'

'I don't think that's it,' Luke said. 'I think he is genuinely heartbroken at losing his wife.'

'Do we know who does Mrs Leaming's garden?' I asked, as the unanswered question popped into my mind.

'George Felton, of course,' Maud answered promptly.

'Could they be in it together?' I mused.

'Let's not forget Joe Noble,' Luke said. 'He wasn't at all happy when he realised you had told me about the illegal alcohol sales he's been making at the pub. Which reminds me.'

He passed a sealed envelope across the table towards me. 'What's that?'

'He said it's what he owed you,' Luke said.

'Do you think that's what it is? Or do you think it's hush money?'

He shrugged. 'Could be either.'

I slid a finger under the flap of the envelope and flipped through the contents. There was enough there to treat me and Ruby to a night out in London with a nice amount left. Perhaps I would treat myself to a new frock.

'Finally there's Ernest Harrington,' I said. 'The Harringtons' nanny said Ernest wasn't at all kind to Elsie and, furthermore, they had arguments about her belief that he was having an affair.'

'Goodness me.' Maud clicked her tongue. 'It seems like the entire village is at it.'

I tried to ignore the pointed look she gave me and Luke, but it didn't stop my cheeks from heating with embarrassment. I remembered the bishop's words the night before and resolved to keep my distance from the vicar as soon as we had solved this case. It wasn't fair for him to be mixed up in gossip. Until such a time as Stan either turned up and gave me a divorce, or his body was found, I had no business having romantic thoughts for another man.

'Nothing is as it seems,' Luke said. 'I thought Mr Harrington was very caring towards his wife on Saturday after Mrs Warren's death.'

'And sometimes things are exactly as they seem,' I said quietly as the final piece of the puzzle slipped into place in my mind. Why had we made things so complicated when the answer was so very simple?

'What is it?'

'I think I know who it is.' I had spoken tentatively, but as soon as I said the words, I was certain. Sometimes things are exactly as they seem.

'You must tell Detective Inspector Robertson at once,' Maud insisted.

'After you've told us, of course!' Luke looked to me for the name of the person I now believed to have committed the murders.

'Oh no, I couldn't tell the detective the name of the person yet,' I said. 'That wouldn't do. We have no evidence, but I know exactly how to get the proof he will need.'

'I don't think I like that look on your face,' Luke said. 'Do you have a plan?'

I got to my feet. 'Yes. I must get into the village before the post office closes.'

'The post office?' Luke raised an eyebrow at me.

'Gossip in this village spreads from a place where people gather. Either the shops or church. If I tell Mrs Rogers I know who the killer is, the entire village will know by the time they sit down to supper.'

'That is the most foolhardy plan I have ever heard,' Luke said. 'You will put yourself at an unacceptable risk of harm!'

'That's the idea.'

'Oh dear,' Maud said. 'I think she's had too much sun. Her brains are addled.'

'Don't you both see? If I say I know who did it, then that person will come and attack me to make sure I don't talk.'

'Your plan is no better for spelling it out in plain English.' Luke shook his head. 'It's a ridiculous notion. I can't allow it.'

'*You* can't allow it?' I bristled at his propriety tone. All thoughts of his masculine forearms flew from my mind faster than Maud's cat fleeing from Lizzie.

'You'll be killed,' he said sullenly.

'Not if I tell Detective Inspector Robertson my scheme and he stations police officers in my house to catch the killer.'

'And if they're too late and you get killed?'

'At least you'll know who did it.'

'Don't be flippant.' He strode over to Maud's kitchen door. 'I can't be a part of this. It's one thing investigating these murders, which is dangerous enough, but it's another thing entirely to deliberately put yourself at risk. It's selfish, Martha.'

The door clicked softly closed behind him. I don't know if it was the calm way he departed the house, or the way he said my name, but it left me feeling like I'd just lost something very special.

* * *

Later that evening, while I made supper, I told Ruby about my plan. I explained how I had gone into the village and told Mrs

Rogers that I had asked the police to call on me in the morning so I could explain exactly how I had worked out who the killer was.

'I must say, I have to agree with the vicar. It seems unnecessarily dangerous. Isn't that what we have a police force for?'

'The detective thought my plan was excellent.'

'I expect it will be,' Ruby agreed. 'If you don't die.'

'I won't die,' I reassured her.

'Lizzie will bark the moment someone opens the garden gate.' Ruby's mouth turned up into a grin. 'It won't work.'

'Lizzie will be in your bedroom with you. If the murderer chooses the wrong bedroom, then Lizzie will ensure your safety.'

'How *will* the killer know which bedroom to target?'

'All the cottages in this row are identical. The main bedroom is at the front of the house. The smaller room at the back.'

'Do you think the killer will come tonight?'

'I would, wouldn't you? If you thought someone knew your identity and they made it clear they would speak to the police the next day. The murderer will definitely try to shut me up for good tonight.'

Ruby shuddered. 'I don't know how you can be so calm, Martha. We're talking about your death.'

'I have faith in the police, and it's not like I'd be badly missed.'

'Martha!' Ruby crashed her teacup into the saucer. 'The vicar is right. You *are* selfish. What an awful thing to say. I would miss you. I would miss you terribly.'

'Sorry, that was thoughtless.' I stirred the vegetable soup, then walked over to her and patted her shoulder. 'I'm your sister. Of course you'd miss me.'

'That's not it.' Ruby sounded as though she was going to cry. 'It's not just because you're my sister. It's because you're you. Martha, do you really not have any idea of how very much I admire you?'

'Me?'

'Yes.' She reached up and put a hand over mine. 'I can't imagine having a better big sister.'

'It is *me* who admires *you*,' I told her. 'You know about so many things I can only dream of.'

'Oh,' she said dismissively. 'They are just things. Anyone can learn about make-up, hair and clothes. You care for me in little ways every single day. Goodness, Martha, you even warm my slippers before I get home from work in the middle of the summer.'

'And I shall be here doing the very same thing every day until you marry.'

She snorted. 'That won't be any time soon.'

'Won't it?' I asked, enjoying the emotional connection flowing between the two of us. 'What about that fellow I saw you with on Tuesday on the train platform? He looked awfully keen.'

'I've already told you,' she said sharply. 'He's nobody.'

'But—'

'Can we talk about something else?' She twisted around and smiled at me. 'Not him. And not murders.'

'I'm not sure I remember how to have a conversation that doesn't involve death, poison or killers.'

'I forgot to tell you.' Ruby picked up a teaspoon and idly stirred her tea. 'I saw a woman going into Charles Warren's house when I was walking back from the station.'

'Charles's house, are you sure?'

'Oh yes,' she replied. 'I know I sound just like Mrs Burnett or Mrs Garrett, but I actually stopped walking to watch. He opened the door, kissed her on the cheek, then you'll never guess what he did next.'

'I don't think I will. What did he do?'

'Took a suitcase from her and took her into the house. In broad daylight. How brazen is that?'

'Perhaps it was his daughter.'

'Martha, you know the Warrens didn't have children. We've lived in Westleham long enough to know that.'

I walked back over to the Aga. Ruby's revelation left me feeling rather sad. I had truly believed that Charles loved Alice. Now it seemed like Mrs Burnett was right and everyone in the village was sneaking around with someone else.

* * *

I sat in the chair at the foot of my bed. When my bedroom was opened, the killer would see my empty bed. Hopefully, the distance would give the police time to jump out and apprehend the vicious poisoner before they had time to harm me.

The church clock chimed three in the morning. My eyes stung from keeping them open so long past my usual bedtime, but I dared not close them. Even though there were police in my bedroom with me, downstairs in the parlour, and another with Ruby, I was still terrified, despite my earlier bravado.

I thought I heard a noise outside, but I'd been sure I'd heard something at least a dozen times already. Holding my breath, as though that would make my hearing keener, I strained to hear if the faint sound came again. A soft click told me that someone had just closed my garden gate.

My heart hammered louder than the commuter train to London and I thought I might be sick. My stomach felt as though it was lodged in my lungs, making it hard to take a deep breath.

Terror made it difficult to discern what were real sounds and what were those made up by my terrified mind. There was no doubting the creaking of the third stair from the top. It seemed to echo around the quiet house. My feet were cold, even though they were encased in my slippers. I wondered if I would be able to move if I needed to, or if I would be too frightened, or my muscles would protest after sitting in one place for so long.

The doorknob on my bedroom door jiggled, and I wanted to squeeze my eyes shut. It was too late to back out now. The reality was more terrifying than I had imagined. Worse than any nightmare I'd ever experienced.

The door slowly opened, and I closed my fingers around the torch in my dressing-gown pocket. As soon as the dark-clothed figure eased into my bedroom, I pressed down on the button and raised the light directly into the intruder's surprised face.

He grabbed a pillow from my bed and, in a flash, covered my face. I tried to scream, but no sound would come.

I reached out with the torch and aimed it in the direction of Ernest Harrington's head. A resounding crack told me I had hit my mark. The pillow fell from my face, and when I opened my eyes again, my bedroom was full of police officers.

I had known the man who was coming to kill me that night would be Ernest Harrington but I was surprised at how shocked I was when his familiar features leaned down over me and pushed the pillow into my face.

'Martha?' Ruby's voice sounded like it was coming from a long way off. 'Darling? Are you all right?'

'Yes,' I said, then burst into noisy sobs.

Someone turned on the main bedroom light, and Ruby was at my side, her arms around me. She murmured comforting words and stroked my hair. Which made me cry harder. How had I reached the grand old age of thirty-three before someone had showed me real affection?

Heavy footsteps sounded on the wooden stairs and Detective Inspector Robertson came into the room. 'Are you all right, Mrs Miller? You were incredibly brave.'

'Not just that,' Ruby said. 'She whacked him on the head. My sister is a hero.'

'Yes, Miss Andrews, she is.'

'Is he dead?' I peered over Ruby's shoulder.

'No, just unconscious.'

'Shame,' Ruby said savagely.

'He was going to suffocate me,' I whispered.

'We would never have let him get that far,' the detective said.

'He had the pillow over my face,' I said indignantly. 'Believe me, at that point I thought the vicar was right, and I was completely insane for suggesting this hare-brained scheme.'

'All's well that ends well.' Ruby pulled a handkerchief out of her dressing-gown pocket and passed it to me.

'Get cuffs on him.' The detective pointed at Ernest, and a uniformed officer jumped forward to follow orders. 'The last thing we want is him regaining consciousness and trying to make a run for it. I'm far too tired to chase him through the village.'

'Goodness, look at me. I can't stop shaking.' I held my hands in front of my face.

'You need a hot cup of tea,' Ruby said decisively. 'Let's get Lizzie and go into the kitchen. I shall make a pot of proper tea.'

'We can't—'

'We jolly well can,' she argued. 'If we can't have a cup of strong sweet tea after the night we've had, when can we?'

'But our rations won't last if we—'

'Martha, I'll not hear another word about it!'

Ruby pulled me to my feet. We stepped around a prone Ernest Harrington and towards the bedroom door.

'Thank you, Mrs Miller.' Detective Inspector Robertson reached out a hand and placed it on my arm. 'I will be back in the morning to wrap things up properly.'

'It *is* morning,' Ruby said derisively.

'Later, when you've had time to rest.'

His ears were pink, and a faint flush dusted his cheekbones.

'Please thank your colleagues for me,' I said. 'I felt safer with them in the house.'

'You didn't need them though, did you?' Ruby squeezed my arm. 'I'm so very proud of you.'

15

The following morning, Mrs Garrett, Mrs Burnett, and I were sitting in the kitchen when Detective Inspector Robertson returned. Ruby had gone off to work as usual, despite having no sleep whatsoever.

'Has he confessed?'

'He's refusing to talk,' the detective said.

'Who?' Mrs Burnett and Mrs Garrett asked in unison.

'Haven't you told them who it was?' the detective asked with a laugh.

'I wanted to wait until you got here so I only had to go through the story once.' I walked over to the kitchen window and looked out. There was no sign of Luke. I hoped he would come over this morning to see how things turned out, but he must have had something better to do. It was pointless being bitter. The vicar wasn't for me. It showed good sense on his part that he hadn't come over.

'Right, Mrs Miller, where shall you start?'

'I want to know how you worked out who it was,' Maud said.

'Don't be ridiculous,' Ada said. 'A story starts at the beginning, not at the end.'

'I couldn't have worked it out without you both.' I smiled at Maud and Ada. 'You were both quite magnificent.'

'Yes, we were, rather, weren't we?' Maud looked at the detective. 'Luckily for you.'

'I'll start at the show,' I said. 'At the time, I thought someone who had a specific motive had deliberately killed Mrs Warren.'

'Wasn't she killed on purpose?' Ada asked.

'No,' I said. 'That is the killer wanted to kill *someone,* but it didn't matter to them *who* they killed.'

'I don't think I understand.' Maud frowned.

'I didn't either. Not for many days. Then suddenly the answer was there, and it was so blindingly obvious I felt foolish for not seeing it straight away.'

'In that case, I must be incredibly stupid. I was there with you last night when you arrived at your conclusion, and I still don't see it.'

Reaching into the centre of the table, I retrieved my notes. 'I started thinking the killer must have a reason to kill Alice. See here where I completed these columns? The only person who had a real motive for killing Alice was her husband.' I flipped over the page. 'But then he had no motive for killing Elsie.'

'Did anyone have a motive for killing Elsie?' Edith asked.

'Joe Noble had one, but it was very weak.'

The detective frowned. 'Did he? I don't think you shared that information with me.'

I looked down at the piece of paper in my hand. 'If it's all the same to you, I'd rather keep that between Joe and me.'

'Does it have any relevance to the investigation?'

'None.'

'I will accept that,' he said. 'Go on.'

'When it comes to the last column, there were so many people who had the opportunity to kill both women, it was difficult to work out what were important facts and what was just ordinary village life. It's very rare for someone not to have a secret. Once I uncovered those, it opened up motives. People will often kill to keep their private lives just that.'

'What's this about Sheraton?' Maud asked.

'I think I can answer that,' Ada said. 'It has something to do with the fellow you asked me about, doesn't it? Arthur Wade?'

A look of disgust flashed across the detective's face. 'A truly disgusting crime. What sort of person can loot bombed houses?'

Maud tutted. 'Vermin. That's who.'

'How is that connected to the investigation?'

'That was from the information you gave me, Mrs Garrett. It was very useful. Once we knew Arthur Wade was financing Mrs Leaming's house, it became imperative to find out who he was and why he would pay for a house he didn't live in.'

'Fancy Mrs Leaming being in cahoots with a criminal.' Maud shook her head. 'What a disgrace.'

'She wasn't directly involved in the offences,' Detective Inspector Robertson told us. 'We believe there was a gang of men who carried out the thefts. Mrs Leaming posed as a war widow and kept the stolen items in her home. Every now and again, Mr Wade, or one of his accomplices, would take a piece of furniture and sell it. They were careful not to sell the items in the same area in which they were taken.'

'But he was imprisoned?' Ada wore a particularly sour look.

'He was caught red-handed robbing a house in nineteen forty-four,' the detective confirmed. 'It wasn't until we went through Mrs Leaming's house that we could pin a number of other offences onto him. He'll go back inside for a lot longer than two years this time.'

'They should throw away the key,' Ada said with feeling.

Maud tapped the paper in front of me. 'So Alice knew the sideboard in Mrs Leaming's house was a Sheraton?'

'I don't know if she was sure, but she at least suspected, and Mrs Leaming knew Alice was onto her.'

'She could have killed her to keep her quiet so she and the Wade chap could carry on selling their stolen furniture.'

'Yes, but then I couldn't uncover any reason for her wanting Elsie out of the way. It made no sense. The murders just didn't seem to have any common thread except, of course, for the way they were killed.'

'What about George?'

'The detective was adamant George did not have the opportunity to kill either woman. He wasn't anywhere near the marquee immediately prior to Alice's death, and he wasn't even in the village when Elsie died. However, the vicar and I realised the killer didn't need to be nearby when the women were killed. He simply needed to have poisoned their drink.'

'Poison could have been added to Elsie's bottle of gin at any time, and George was always there doing the garden. I never did trust that man.'

'And what's this about the beans?'

'I realised from Alice's committee notes that Mr West claimed the garden saboteur destroyed his broad beans. However, he won first prize for them at the show. Was that really enough reason for him to kill Alice, though? I wasn't sure.'

Ada picked up the teapot and topped up everyone's cup. 'Whoever killed Alice could have killed Elsie to keep her quiet. Maybe she found something out and had to be silenced.'

'Let's look at Charles,' I said. 'As soon as we heard he had a large insurance policy on Alice's life, it seemed likely he was the culprit. I'm a little embarrassed to admit that the vicar and I followed him to London to try and catch him with the girlfriend we understood he was involved with.'

'Did you catch him?' Ada asked.

'No, there's no girlfriend.'

'Good, I rather like Mr Warren. He was a good husband to Alice. Very attentive and hard working.'

'Ruby saw a lady go into his house yesterday evening, but the detective has informed me that is his sister. So a monetary reason for killing his wife and none for Elsie.'

'Who's left?'

'Ernest Harrington.'

'Was it him?' Maud leaned forward, her face flushed with excitement.

'Yes, it was.'

Ada shook her head. 'I don't understand. This is the other way around to Alice's murder. I can see why he might want to kill his own wife, but why would he want to kill Alice?'

'As I said earlier, he didn't. He wanted to kill *someone*. The who didn't matter. When Florence told the vicar that the drinks had been prepared before she started serving them, it made me realise Alice's death was a random crime. It was carried out to create a smokescreen for the murderer's actual intent.'

'Oh, that's wicked,' Maud murmured. 'Poor Alice. And poor Charles.'

'Why did he want his wife dead?'

'He was almost certainly having an affair.'

'You don't know?' the detective queried, a puzzled look on his handsome face. 'I thought you were sure of your reasoning. That's why I agreed to last night's charade.'

'I was as sure as I could be.' I finished my tea. For once, I didn't care that our rations were running low. Who cared about things like that after the week I'd had? 'It was the only thing that made sense. Mrs Rogers suggested Ernest spent a lot of time in the pub, the nanny was asked to send letters to someone in Edgecumbe, and Joe Noble's weekend barmaid is from that village.'

'That's an incredible leap.' The detective rubbed a hand across his jaw.

'It is,' I agreed. 'But it all fitted together. Last night when we were discussing what I had learned from Nancy Turner, the vicar commenting that nothing was as it seemed, I had the thought that sometimes things *are* exactly as they seem. This case was just so. A man who killed because he had found a woman he wanted more than his wife.'

'It's rather clever,' Ada said. 'In an incredibly evil way, of course.'

'What will you do now, Mrs Miller?'

'I rather think, Mrs Burnett, that I might take a blanket into the garden and have a nap in the sun.'

'Goodness, how decadent!' Ada remarked. Her face broke into a wide smile.

'I should get on and see how things are going over at Mrs Leaming's house,' the detective said. 'I will come back later to let you know.'

'I shall expect you around six, shall I?'

'Um... yes. It may well be around that time.'

'What a coincidence.'

'I'll see you out.'

As we approached the front door, he caught hold of my elbow. 'I mean to ask your sister to go out on a date with me.'

'Are you asking my permission?'

'Do I need your permission?'

'I'm not her mother,' I said, enjoying his discomfort.

'Nevertheless, I would like your agreement. Ruby lives here with you. It seems only right I ask you.'

'You seem a very nice fellow,' I told him. 'But the decision is my sister's. She can be quite headstrong, as I'm sure you have realised.'

He grinned. 'I rather like that about her.'

* * *

Later that evening, the door knocker sounded only moments after Ruby had got home from work.

'Goodness me, he's keener than I thought!'

'Who?' Ruby asked, a puzzled look on her pretty face.

'Never mind.' I hurried out of the kitchen to answer the door. 'You didn't waste any... Oh, goodness. Who are you?'

The man on the doorstep looked vaguely familiar. 'Is this the right house for Ruby? You must be Martha.'

I didn't like his overfamiliar tone. 'I am Ruby's sister, Mrs Miller. And you are?'

'Phillip. Phillip Hardacre. I work with Ruby.'

'Do you indeed?' I finally realised where I had seen this man before. 'You were on the platform at Slough on Tuesday morning. I saw you manhandling my sister.'

He peered over my shoulder. 'If I could just come in—'

'No.' I shook my head for extra emphasis. 'You cannot. I don't know you, and what I do know of you I don't like.'

'Ruby!' he called. 'Ruby, I must see you! Please, Ruby!'

I tried to push the door closed, but he stuck a foot in the way. Ruby walked down the hallway and stood behind me. 'Go away, Phillip. I've told you. It's over.'

'Is there a problem here?' The welcome voice of Detective Inspector Robertson floated down the path. He covered the short distance of the path with his long-legged strides. 'Is this man bothering you, Mrs Miller?'

'He's come to see Ruby, but he wouldn't leave when I asked him to.'

The detective towered over Phillip Hardacre, whose face had turned sulky. Phillip put out a hand and grabbed Ruby's arm. 'Please, come and talk to me!'

'If you want to keep that hand, you'd be wise to remove it from the young lady's arm. Immediately!' the detective growled.

Phillip dropped it and stepped back. He was handsome in a smarmy, conceited sort of way. All polished shoes, too much pomade and overconfidence. 'I don't know what all the fuss is about. I only wanted to talk to her.'

'Pleasant young men do not call at a young lady's house with a disrespectful attitude and not leave when asked,' I said sharply.

'I love your sister.' A stubborn look passed over his face.

Ruby sighed. 'Phillip, you're *married*.'

'Ruby!' I couldn't stop the disappointment in my tone as I turned to face her. 'How could you have a relationship with a married man?'

Tears filled her eyes. 'I didn't know he was married. As soon as I did, I ended things, but he can't take no for an answer. He follows me about, waits for my train to get into Slough and makes an absolute pest of himself.'

'Come on.' Detective Inspector Robertson caught hold of Phillip's elbow and walked him to the path. 'If I find out you have been anywhere near this young lady again, I shall have you arrested for breaching the peace. Now get along with you.'

'Thank you, Inspector.'

'I don't think you'll be having any trouble from him again, Miss Andrews, but if you do, please let me know and I will deal with him.'

'Come along into the kitchen and I will make you a cup of tea,' she said. 'Milk and two sugars, isn't it?'

'How do you know that?'

I looked at the detective and, sure enough, the tops of his ears were pink again. Ruby had thawed towards him considerably, and remembering the way he took his tea was a definite sign that she liked the good-looking detective.

'I remembered,' she said shyly. I never would have believed it if I hadn't heard it with my own ears. If I hadn't just heard her speak, I wouldn't have believed that Ruby would ever act coyly. 'Do you want a cup, Martha?'

'Not for me, thank you. I've had so much tea this week I don't think I could look at another cup.'

'Did you enjoy your nap in the sun, Mrs Miller?'

'I couldn't sleep,' I confessed. 'Last night's events were still swirling around in my head.'

That wasn't entirely the truth. I was afraid that if I fell asleep in the garden, I wouldn't hear Luke when he came over to talk to me about the case, as he surely would. But he hadn't. The last time I'd seen him was the previous evening when he left Maud's kitchen. It seemed silly to think of missing someone that you'd known for less than a week, but I regretted the loss of his company.

'Let's sit outside,' Ruby said. 'It's much cooler now.'

I went into the parlour and grabbed the blanket from the back of the sofa. 'Let's go.'

Ruby and I stretched the blanket on the small area of grass and sat down. The detective stood awkwardly facing us, his back to the garden gate at the side of the house.

'I'd like to speak to your sister now,' he said.

'Fabulous. Don't let me stop you.'

'To ask her what we spoke about earlier.'

'Yes, I remember,' I said. 'Do carry on.'

'Miss Andrews.' He grabbed his hat from his head and twisted it round in his hands. Ruby looked at me in confusion. I smiled at her and then gave the detective an encouraging nod.

As I looked back at him, I saw Luke approaching the garden gate. 'I wondered if you would like to come to the pictures with me tomorrow night. I can pick you up in my motor car.'

Luke turned and headed back around the side of the house. I could have called him back and explained that the detective was asking Ruby, who was out of Luke's sight, on a date and not me, but I didn't. It was probably for the best that I didn't encourage him to spend time with me.

'That sounds very nice,' Ruby said carefully. 'I would like that very much.'

'How lovely. You'll take good care of my sister, Inspector, and have her home at a reasonable hour?'

'Martha!' Ruby squeaked. 'You're embarrassing me.'

'Am I really?'

She looked at me and we both dissolved into giggles.

'What am I to call you?' Ruby asked.

'What? I don't understand.'

'Tomorrow, silly,' she responded. 'I can't call you "Inspector" while we're out, can I?'

'Oh, I see. Now the case has finished, you should call me Ben.'

'You must call me Martha,' I said. 'Now come and sit down, you're giving me a crick in my neck staring up at you.'

Ruby and I shuffled closer together to make room. She grabbed my hand and squeezed it. Tears of happiness filled my eyes. My sister and I were closer than ever. There were two women in the village that I thought I could call my friends. In the past, I'd only ever had acquaintances, never real friends.

Lizzie bounded over and licked my face. I was luckier than so many people, despite my troubles with Stan. The sadness I felt as Luke walked away would fade. Tomorrow, I would carry on with my normal life – gardening, the village committee and caring for the house and Ruby.

There would be no more long talks with the vicar about suspects, motives and our attempts at investigation. I would always be grateful for this last week when I could forget, even for brief moments, that I was an abandoned wife with a stiflingly boring life.

'Do you have to drive home this evening?' Ruby asked Ben suddenly.

'No, I didn't come over in my car today.'

'Are you officially off duty?'

'Yes.'

She jumped up and grabbed his cup out of his hands. 'I'm throwing this tea away. My sister has just solved a double murder. That calls for her very best plum gin!'

She raced inside and returned with a bottle of tonic, the gin and three glasses. 'What an excellent idea, Ruby, thank you.'

Ruby filled our glasses. 'To my sister, the sleuth, cheers!'

I couldn't remember a time when I was happier. I grinned at her. 'Cheers!'

MORE FROM CATHERINE COLES

We hope you enjoyed reading *Poison at the Village Show*. If you did, please leave a review.

If you'd like to gift a copy, this book is also available as an ebook, digital audio download and audiobook CD.

Sign up to Catherine Cole's mailing list for news, competitions and updates on future books.

https://bit.ly/CatherineColesNews

ABOUT THE AUTHOR

The daughter of a military father, Catherine was born in Germany and lived most of the first 14 years of her life abroad. She spent her school years devouring everything her school library had to offer!

Her favourites were romance and mysteries. Her love for the Nancy Drew books led Catherine to check out every mystery story she could find. She soon found Agatha Christie, whose writing Catherine describes as 'brilliantly genius'.

Catherine writes cosy mysteries that take place in the English countryside. Her extremely popular Tommy & Evelyn Christie mysteries are set in 1920s North Yorkshire.

Catherine lives in northeast England with her two spoiled dogs who have no idea they are not human!

Visit Catherine's Website:

https://catherinecoles.com

Follow Catherine on social media:

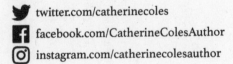

twitter.com/catherinecoles
facebook.com/CatherineColesAuthor
instagram.com/catherinecolesauthor

ABOUT BOLDWOOD BOOKS

Boldwood Books is a fiction publishing company seeking out the best stories from around the world.

Find out more at www.boldwoodbooks.com

Sign up to the Book and Tonic newsletter for news, offers and competitions from Boldwood Books!

http://www.bit.ly/bookandtonic

We'd love to hear from you, follow us on social media:

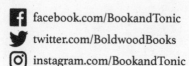

facebook.com/BookandTonic

twitter.com/BoldwoodBooks

instagram.com/BookandTonic